Protective Custody

Zach Peckens

NEWMAN SPRINGS PUBLISHING
320 Broad Street
Red Bank, NJ 07701

First originally published by Newman Springs Publishing 2021

ISBN 978-1-63692-516-5 (Paperback)
ISBN 978-1-63692-517-2 (Digital)

Printed in the United States of America

The Social Worker

Stephanie Lambert worked for the Department of Children and Family Protective Services and was one of the sharpest and hard-working social workers in the city. She was thirty-three years old, five feet, seven inches, and had red hair, complete with hazel eyes.

Stephanie has been a social worker for four years now. She was persistent with her work and passionate about helping unfortunate kids and families. Her caseload was beyond normal. There weren't enough social workers to handle the loads of all the cases that were brought into DCFPS.

Stephanie had a dark past. She was heavy into drugs and alcohol and partied a lot. She fell into the wrong crowd in high school and was in a downward spiral ever since.

The one event that changed her life around was when she gave birth to her son six years earlier. She was in no state to raise a child. The hardest thing she could ever do was to give him up for adoption. She didn't remember much about him. After that day, she decided to go to rehab and get herself clean. She then applied to become a social worker to help others in need.

With only eight social workers in the Bureau of Manhattan, Stephanie, along with her colleagues, were very overworked. Stephanie alone had nineteen active cases to herself. Her friend, Michelle Parker, had nearly two dozen open cases on her workload.

The DCFPS had some cruel and grueling cases they had to deal with. From drug-dealing parents of little children who were so malnourished that they were hospitalized to stepfathers sleeping in the same bed with their young kids. They didn't make many friends but a lot of enemies doing this line of work. From open threats to hate mail, Stephanie and her colleagues were dedicated to helping children and their families.

Her desk was piled high with case files. She had to document when she saw the families and children and had to make sure the house was clean and safe for the kids. If anything was out of place, such as no food in the house, Stephanie had to be the bad guy and ask the parents why.

Stephanie and Michelle spent their entire day at their desks, doing paperwork. The other six social workers were making house visits. She looked through her case files and put her information into the DCFPS database—her house visits, complaints filed toward the families, and interviews, among other things, she had to document. As she was logging all her notes, she couldn't help but notice the complaints on some of her cases.

One case file was about a single mother who was working two jobs to help support her three kids. Her husband died in a car wreck last year. One of her kid's teachers complained to DCFPS that the child's clothes were filthy. Stephanie was duty-bound to investigate. The other claimed that she was very overworked and tired and tried so hard to make sure that she has food on the table for her kids.

Another case was of a mother using drugs. She was arrested twice for possession. The child was taken away from her. She fought with DCFPS to get him back. She made three house visits within the last six months. She was using again and lived in unhealthy conditions. She reported this and was threatened by the mother that she was couldn't keep her away from her child.

It was 5:00 PM when Stephanie decided to call it a night. She had been up for thirty hours straight. Most of her paper was filed and up-to-date in the database. She thought to herself that she could come in early tomorrow and get it finished. She turned off her computer and desk lamp. As she was getting ready to walk out the door, her boss, Todd Markus, came out from his office.

"Oh, good you didn't leave yet," Todd said. He was in his fifties and was the supervisor for over fifteen years. He assigns the cases to the social workers as they come in. Todd was pudgy and was partially bald with glasses.

"Can't this wait until tomorrow, Todd? I'm very exhausted," Stephanie pleaded with him.

"No, it can't," he replied.

They both walked back to this office. She sat in front of his nice clean desk. Stephanie looked at it and was disgusted. Every social worker has a messy desk and there's disorganization everywhere. Todd's desk was so clean you could eat off it. He sat behind his desk and had a case file sitting in front of him. She looked at it and knew he was going to assign her a new case.

"I have a new case for you," Todd said.

"What is it?" she asked.

"A teacher at Martin Luther King Jr. Elementary School told us that one of her students, Tyler Martin, was absent from her class three days in a row. She tried to call his parents, but there was no answer."

"What's the parents' story?" Stephanie asked.

"We don't know," Todd replied. "The teacher never met them. I asked if she noticed any abnormal behavior from the kid. She said he was very shy and seemed distraught. He was very antisocial and didn't make any friends."

"Sounds like possible neglect," Stephanie said to her boss. She had a date tonight and didn't want to blow it off. It was the first time since her sobriety that she went out to socialize. She didn't want to turn down a possibly abused child who's been missing for three days from school. She reached out her hand reluctantly and said, "I'll take it."

"Great!" Todd said to her. He handed her the case file and said, "I'll call the NYPD and have a patrol car meet her at the residence."

Stephanie wasn't thrilled to accept yet another case with her workload already reaching full capacity. She didn't want to leave a possible neglected child out there while she went out on a date, especially with a short-staffed overworked department.

Stephanie walked back to her desk with a disgruntled look on her face. She sighed loudly and sat down at her desk. Her friend

Michelle noticed she was in a foul mood. Social workers were never in a happy mood, but Stephanie was more down the normal.

"What did he do? Give you another case or something?" Michelle asked Stephanie sarcastically.

"He did," Stephanie replied with a hint of sadness in her voice.

"Why in the hell would you say yes?" Michelle asked. "He does this all the time. He sweet-talks us into taking case after case with no regard to us or our mental or physical well-beings."

"I'm a sucker for punishment," Stephanie replied.

"What about your date tonight?" Michelle curiously asked.

"I can still make it. I'll call him from the road and tell him I may be late," Stephanie replied.

"You just met this guy," Michelle said. "Maybe it's for the best. He could be a serial killer for all you know."

Stephanie didn't say anything. She didn't know much about this guy she was going out with. Michelle was right and was looking out for her friend. Stephanie was scared of having a serious relationship or even having a man to talk to.

"Well, just be careful," Michelle said to her friend.

"Don't worry, I'll tell you all about it tomorrow," Stephanie said as she got her purse and folder and left the office.

House Visit

Stephanie walked out of the office and caught a cab. She told the driver the address and proceeded to the destination. She was not looking forward to going to this kid's residence. As much as she loved helping others, she always felt like the bad person if she were the one taking a kid away from their parents.

Stephanie got out her cell phone and made a call. It was to her date tonight, Derek. She tried her to not break their date tonight. He was very understanding of her situation. She was relieved that maybe she could maybe both be able to meet her new clients and have a nice outing tonight.

It was after five o'clock when Stephanie got to the address in the file. There was an NYPD squad car waiting in front of the building. There were two patrol officers occupied in the car. It was a rough neighborhood. The projects were infested with crime and violence.

Any time a social worker makes a house call, they are always escorted by a police officer to sure their safety. There have been incidents where social workers have had guns and knives pulled on them for just making routine inspections.

Stephanie got out of the taxi and paid the driver. She looked up at the apartment building. It was an old beat-up building. There were a few young teenagers next to the building playing basketball. There was a homeless man sitting next to the apartment building. He had ragged clothes and no shoes on. It was a bad neighborhood.

The two NYPD officers got out of the car and met Stephanie in front of the building. She had her purse, which contained a can of mace. She also had Tyler's file from DCFPS. "Are you from DCFPS?" one of the officers asked.

"Yes!" Stephanie replied. "I'm Stephanie Lambert here to check the well-being of Tyler Martin. The file says his family lives on the third floor of this building."

"I'm officer Hemmingway. This is officer Wilson."

Officer Hemmingway was a four-year decorated officer. He was young and went by the rules. He was straight as they come. Officer Wilson was on the job just over two years now. He was strict about police procedures and policies.

"We'll escort you to the apartment, Ms. Lambert," Officer Wilson said.

Stephanie looked up at the building and sighed loudly. She walked into the building. Officers Wilson and Hemmingway walked right behind her. They walked up to the receptionist's desk. The man sitting behind the desk was typical for being in these parts. He was about three-hundred-plus pounds. His white tank top shirt had stains on it. He was covered in potato chip crumbs.

He was glued to a small TV on the desk in front of him. A man could have thrown a grenade in the lobby, and he wouldn't have even noticed. Stephanie just stood there at the desk, waiting to be noticed.

Hemmingway and Wilson looked at each other, waiting for a response. Stephanie kept standing there, hoping that the bum behind the desk would acknowledge their presence. Finally, Stephanie was impatient and decided to make the first move.

"Excuse me?" Stephanie said to the man behind the desk.

There was no response from the man. He was concentrated on the TV he was watching and chewing on a toothpick. Officer Hemmingway decided he should try to get his attention.

"Hey, buddy!" he said as he raised his voice to the man. Again, no response. This man was in his own world. Finally, Officer Wilson walked over to the desk and took out his baton and started banging it on the desk. The bum nearly jumped out of his chair when he did that.

"WHAT THE HELL!" he yelled to them.

"Do you know if there was anybody in room 3B?" Stephanie asked the bum in an irritated tone of voice.

"I don't keep track of who comes and goes," The bum said back to Stephanie.

"I can see you're too busy doing a lot of nothing to notice much of anything," Officer Hemmingway said to the man behind the desk.

"Thank you for your help," Stephanie said to the bum and walked toward the elevators.

Hemmingway and Wilson walked behind Stephanie to the elevators. There were two elevators next to each other. One of them had an Out of Order sign hanging off the door. They waited for the elevator, which took forever, it seemed like.

Stephanie was looking around at the lobby as they waited. There were cigarettes all over the floor. The trash can was overflowed. She was disgusted that the thought of a kid living in these conditions going through her head.

They got onto the elevator finally. The officers got in behind her. Officer Wilson pushed the button marked three on the elevator wall. They stood there as they reached the third floor. Stephanie was about to get off the elevator when Officer Hemmingway stopped her. He got off the elevator first and looked to make it was safe.

Stephanie followed Hemmingway, and Wilson was the last off the elevator. She went to the right, down the hallway. She was terrified to see what was on the other side of 3B. They could hear loud music coming from one of the apartments.

They got to the apartment. The door was cracked open. Stephanie knocked on the door. There was no answer. Officer Wilson knocked on the wall next to the door. "NYPD! OPEN UP!" Officer Wilson yelled. Again, there was no response. Hemmingway walked up to the door and slowly opened it.

"Don't you need a warrant to go in there?" Stephanie asked.

"Nope. We are checking on the well-being of a child. The door was opened. Probable cause made us believe that a child could be in danger," Hemmingway replied.

Both Hemmingway and Wilson unsnapped the safety straps from their side arms and slowly walked into the apartment. The carpets were filthy. The walls had holes in them. The odor coming from the inside of the apartment was related to a garbage dump.

"NYPD! ANYBODY HOME!" Wilson yelled.

There was no answer. They could hear the sound of the TV in the background. Nobody seemed to be in the apartment. They slowly made their way into the living room area. There were no signs of human life.

Stephanie walked toward the couch and saw the top of a little blond boy's head. It was Tyler Martin. He was sitting on the couch, watching *SpongeBob SquarePants*. He was wearing a Scooby-Doo T-shirt and shorts. He had a bloodied nose.

She sat next to him on the couch. "Are you Tyler?" she asked him. He didn't say anything back to her. He just sat there with tears in his eyes, staring at Stephanie. She reached into her purse and took out a pack of tissues. She handed one to him. He slowly took it from her hands and applied it to his nose.

There was a noise coming from the back of the apartment. Hemmingway and Wilson drew their guns and slowly went back to the bedrooms. Hemmingway kicked open the door. There was a heavyset hair-covered man having sex with an unconscious woman. "NYPD! FREEZE!" Wilson yelled at the man.

Hemmingway pulled him off the comatose woman and threw him to the ground. He cuffed the man. He seems either intoxicated or high on some drugs. Wilson went over to check the woman for a pulse. It was faint, but she was still alive. Wilson then radioed in for a drug team and an ambulance.

Stephanie overheard the commotion in the back. She put her hand on Tyler's back for comfort. He was so traumatized that he couldn't even accept her embrace. She knew that he was mistreated like this for a while now. Her heart melted for him.

She left him on the couch and walked over to the kitchen to get him something to drink. There was dust on the counters. She opened the refrigerator to give Tyler something to drink. There was nothing in the fridge at all. No food or anything to drink.

She checked the cupboards to see if there was any food there. There wasn't anything in the apartment to eat or drink. There were cobwebs on the cookware under the oven. There was a rat crawling around under the sink.

Hemmingway came out from the back of the apartment with the man in cuffs. He put shorts on the suspect to avoid scaring the public away with his nudity. He took him down and put him in his squad car.

Wilson was helping the woman who was unconscious to the floor. She had track marks on her arms. It looked like an overdose to Officer Wilson. His first guess would be a heroin overdose. Her pulse was faint, and she was hardly breathing.

Stephanie couldn't stand seeing this poor kid being mistreated like that. She went over to Tyler and sat next to him. "You want to come with me, Tyler?" she compassionately asked. Again, he didn't say a word to her.

She extended her hand out to him. He looked at it with blood still dripping from his nose. He reached out his hand and grabbed hers. She smiled at him. She thought that her parents or whoever was not taking care of him had smiled at him before. They stood up together and walked slowly out of the apartment.

They walked out of the building and sat on the bench next to the entrance. She put her coat on Tyler. The fall weather was fast approaching. Tyler stared at the man sitting in the squad car. Tyler looked like he has seen a ghost. Stephanie saw Tyler and the man staring at each other. She covered his eyes and turned his head to avoid looking at him.

The ambulance showed up. The EMTs quickly got the gurney out of the back and raced into the building. Another squad car showed up as well. Hemmingway was talking to the other officer who had just arrived. Stephanie was just scared for Tyler, yet thankful that she took his case.

Hemmingway walked over to Stephanie and Tyler. "This is Officer Velero. He is going to take you guys to Mercy for a checkup."

She stood up and reached out for Tyler's hand. He was still holding a tissue to his bloodied nose. He then reached his bloodied hand out to her. He stood up and walked with her to Velero's car.

The Checkup

They got to Mercy General around 7:00 PM. Like any typical day in the emergency room, it was packed. Officer Velero escorted Stephanie and Tyler through the ER. The staff knew that they were coming. They had a room ready for Tyler. The ER physician told Stephanie to wait outside the room while they examined him properly.

She went outside and called Todd. She told him about how horrible living conditions Tyler was living under. "It was the worst case I've ever seen since I've been with DCFPS!" she told Todd. She was worried for him. He was mistreated, abused physically, and who knows what else.

"After his checkup and your paperwork, turn him over to St. Catherine's Home," Todd said to Stephanie.

She felt even more horrible than before. She didn't want to just hand him over to a home filled with strangers. He needed love and care. She felt different about Tyler than any other case she had ever worked on before.

Stephanie walked back into the ER to check on Tyler. Officers Hemmingway and Wilson were there. They had rushed the woman from the apartment to Mercy General. She walked over to them in the middle of the chaos. "Thank you so much for coming with me," Stephanie said to them.

"How is the boy?" Hemmingway asked.

"I don't know. They haven't let me back to see him yet." She stood there with her arms crossed. Stephanie was very concerned about Tyler's well-being.

"Do you know anything about the man or woman in the apartment with Tyler?"

"Amy Martin was identified as the woman. We found her wallet in the apartment. She adopted Tyler when he was two years old. She had a job as a bank teller. Then got fired over a year ago and has been dealing with drugs ever since, according to the track marks we saw." Wilson informed Stephanie of her record.

Stephanie was distraught that nobody had really taken care of Tyler in over a year at least. She didn't know how to handle it. This wasn't any other DCFPS case. She felt different about this one. She felt connected to Tyler in some way.

The ER physician came walking out of the room. "I'm Dr. Paxton. Are you with DCFPS?" Dr. Paxton was a middle-aged female doctor. She was very compassionate about kids.

"Yes. I'm the one who found him. How is he?" she desperately asked.

"He's lucky. We're going to X-ray his nose. It's red and swollen, but I don't think there are any fractures. He's malnourished and dehydrated. We started a bag of fluids and going to feed him so he can get his strength up. No signs of other physical or sexual abuse."

She was so relieved to hear that. No massive damage was performed on this kid. She waited for him to come back from radiology. She called her date, Derek, to let him know that they may have to postpone.

Derek was understanding about what her situation was and about her job. He still wanted to see her. He didn't mind waiting later to see her. She was relieved to hear that too. She didn't expect him to stick around long. She rarely had time for anything else other than her work.

Tyler came back from getting his X-rays. She walked into the room. His nose was red and swollen. He didn't say anything to anybody. She didn't want to let him go. She couldn't keep him. All that mattered that he was safe.

She sat on the foot end of the bed. She caressed his legs to comfort him. He still didn't say anything to her. "My name is Stephanie." No response.

Stephanie had a challenge on her hands. She was really concerned about trying to communicate with a terrorized kid. He just sat there in his bed. He had a look of hopelessness on his face. She didn't have the heart to tell Tyler that he was going to be sent to a group home.

She tried to figure out how to make him talk or smile. She got up from the bed. "I'll be right back, Tyler." He didn't even acknowledge Stephanie's remark.

Stephanie quickly left the room and raced across to the other side of the hospital. She was gone for about ten minutes. Tyler kept his head down as he was sitting in his hospital bed. The door opened. It was Stephanie. He didn't even look up to see who it was.

She had something behind her back. "I have something for you," Stephanie said as she sat at the foot end of Tyler's bed. He never did look up at her. Tyler could see a glimpse of something from the corner of his eyes.

It was a light brown teddy bear. He slowly looked up at it. He didn't say anything. Tyler stared at the bear for a minute before slowly reaching out to it. Stephanie handed the bear to him. He took it out of her hands and embraced the bear. Stephanie smiled knowing that she could at least give him something to keep him company and make him feel safe.

It was nearly eight o'clock when Tyler was discharged. Officer Hemmingway walked into the room. It was time to take Tyler to St. Catherine's Group Home. Stephanie didn't want to leave Tyler. It did, however, make her feel better knowing that he would be safe tonight.

"You have to go now, Tyler. They will take good care of you. I will come visit you soon, I promise."

Stephanie was nearly in tears. She slowly got up from Tyler's bed. She put a hospital T-shirt and sweatpants at the foot end of the bed for him to wear.

"Bye, Stephanie!" Tyler said as she was leaving the room. He had finally spoken. Stephanie was so happy to hear his voice. It sounded so little and frail. She walked back over to him and hugged him. He was still holding the teddy bear.

Tears were rolling down her face as she embraced Tyler. She didn't want to let him go. She finally had the courage to let him go and leave the room.

Date Night

Stephanie slowly walked out of Tyler's room. She was distraught. He probably had no care tended to him. He was alone and scared. She never felt this way about any other children before. So why Tyler?

She quickly raced home to get ready for her date with Derek. This will be the first date she has had in years. She was hoping that it would take her mind off Tyler. As worried as she was about Tyler, she was just as nervous about her date with Derek.

They met one day after family court. She was testifying in support of a mother who was trying to gain custody of her daughter back after getting out of rehab. Derek was waiting by the elevators when she came out of the courtroom. They clicked right from the meet. She liked him. Derek felt the same way about her. Now one week later, they were going out on their first date together.

She was racing to get dressed. She got out of the shower and curled her hair. She wanted to impress Derek. It was nearly nine o'clock when she was finally ready. She had on a silk white top, complete with blue jean capris. She slipped put on her white Reebok tennis shoes. Stephanie wasn't much of a fancy dresser, nor did she have anything for such an occasion.

Stephanie met Derek at the theater. He was standing by the ticket office. He was dressed nice. A light-blue dress shirt and black pants. He looked nervous, as if she wasn't going to show up. She took a deep breath and walked over to him. He saw her walking toward him. He smiled in relief that she showed up.

"You look amazing tonight!" Derek was at a loss for words.

"Thank you. So do you." Stephanie was acting like she was at the prom with her high school crush.

They both just stared at each other in silence before going inside. He bought them tickets to see a play. "I hope you don't mind *Romeo and Juliet*," Derek said.

"Not at all," she replied with a smile on her face.

They both walked into the theater. It wasn't as busy as usual. It was the late showing. She didn't mind. Stephanie hated being in a crowded place. The less people, the better. They were seated on the upper balcony. Stephanie had never been to the theater before, let alone the upper balcony.

They managed to sit through the entire showing without falling asleep. It was just after eleven o'clock when the play was over. She felt relieved that she could finally get away from work and not have to worry about the well-being of others. Stephanie finally had time to herself.

"Thank you so much for the wonderful time. I really needed that."

"It was my pleasure," Derek said to Stephanie. They smiled at each other outside of the theater. "Would you like me to give you a ride home?" he asked.

She was hesitant to answer. "I don't mind at all," she finally said.

They walked two blocks over to the parking garage. There weren't many people on the streets. The garage was deserted. They took the steps and walked up to the third level. The stairwell was dark and empty. Stephanie felt safe walking with Derek. She felt like they could be something.

They got to the third level. It was the same as the rest of the garage. There was no sign of any life at all in the garage. Stephanie held onto Derek's arm as they walked over to his car. It was a silver Mercedes Benz.

"Oh shit!" Stephanie said out loud.

'What is it?" Derek asked.

"I must've dropped my wallet somewhere. I'll go back and look for it."

"I'll come with you," Derek suggested to Stephanie.

"It's okay. I'll be quick. Just get the car warmed up and I'll be back. I'm a big girl, don't worry." She winked at him as she walked away.

She quickly went to the stairwell and desperately looked for her wallet. She had her credit cards stolen before, and it was a hassle to get it fixed. She saw her wallet on the stairs just outside the main-level entrance door. She must have dropped it somehow.

Stephanie got back to the third level. She opened the door and could hear other voices. She slowly walked toward Derek's car. She saw him standing there with three other guys. She stood behind a pillar and tried to see and hear what was going on.

It looked like Derek knew the guys that he was talking to. Stephanie thought it could have been a carjacking. But it didn't seem that was the case. She couldn't see any other their faces. They all had their backs turned to her.

"So did you do it yet?" one of the guys asked.

"Not yet. It's complicated," Derek said back.

"It's not complicated at all," another guy said. "We all have our orders. If you don't carry out what you were paid to do, then we will be fucking dead!"

Stephanie was confused about what she was hearing. What was Derek supposed to do?

"I'll get the damn job done, okay?" Derek said to them.

"Well, unfortunately for you, the plans have changed."

Derek looked puzzled. "What do you mean?" he asked.

Stephanie just stood there. She didn't know what to do. Something in her mind was telling her to go out there and interfere. Another part of her was telling her to stay put.

She turned around the pillar and saw one of the guys taking out a knife. He stabbed Derek in the stomach. Stephanie was scared for her life. Derek slowly dropped on the garage floor. The guy still was thrusting the knife into his abdomen.

Another guy turned and saw Stephanie standing there behind one of the pillars. "Hey!" he yelled at her.

She turned and ran to the stairwell door. They started chasing after her. She ran down to the main level. She was trying to flag somebody down, but the road was deserted. There was nobody on the street. She started running up the road toward the theater.

Two of the guys ran out into the street. One of them went down the east side of the road. The other went down the west side of the road. The one guy had the knife he used to stab Derek. The other had a gun with a silencer on it.

Stephanie went down an alley. She didn't know where to go. Her adrenaline was through the roof. The one guy started shooting at Stephanie. She hid behind a dumpster in the alley. "C'mon, lady! We don't want to kill you!"

She could see glaring lights off a building at the end of the alley. Stephanie started running to the street. There were two men coming out of a bar on the corner. She ran up to them. "I just witnessed a murder and I'm next."

It was Detectives Jack Prescott and Dale Harding. They grabbed her and tried to calm her down.

"We're cops. You're safe now!" Dale said to Stephanie.

She was out of breath. She tried to collect herself. "They're after me!" she said to them.

Jack and Dale looked around and didn't see anybody.

Time to Investigate

Jack and Dale walked Stephanie inside the bar. It was near closing time. Cappy was behind the bar. Stephanie has a seat at the end of the bar where Jack always sits. "Call it in, Pop," Jack said to Cappy.

"What the hell is going on, kid?" Cappy asked.

"This girl ran into us outside. She claimed she saw a murder and that she was next. That's all she would say."

"I'll call it in. I'm commanding officer on the scene here. If you do find out anything, you tell me, understand?" Cappy explained to Jack.

They waited at the bar for about fifteen minutes. Stephanie didn't say anything. She was too scared for her life. Jack and Dale were sitting there with her. Cappy sat down a glass of iced water for her. She didn't take it.

Jack sat next to Stephanie. "You should drink that. It will help," Jack said to her. Dale sat on the other side of her.

"I'm Dale. Do you think you can tell us what happened to you?"

Jack leaned over behind Stephanie and nodded his head no to Dale. He could tell that she went through quite an ordeal. Jack could read people. This wasn't like the badger on their last case they worked. This was Jack's expertise. He had a witness to a possible murder. He had to connect with her to help her.

"I think it would help us and help you if you told us your name," Jack said to her in a calm voice.

Jamie came walking around the bar with a blanket. She put it on Stephanie. They were trying to make her feel safe.

"Stephanie Lambert."

They looked at her with a shocked look on their faces. She finally spoke. Even Cappy smiled at the end of the bar.

"Hi, Stephanie. I'm Detective Jack Prescott. That little schoolboy behind you is my partner, Detective Dale Harding."

Jack didn't waste time picking on Dale. Dale even smiled at that comment. Jack was just trying to gain Stephanie's confidence. She leaned her head up and cracked a slight smile from the right corner of her mouth.

"What happened?" Dale bluntly asked her.

She started to cry. She was stronger than she looked. She was trying to hold it together. Most people would have broken down and shut down completely.

"They just killed him," she frantically said.

Dale was writing down what she was saying. "Who is *they*?" Jack asked.

"I don't know. I never saw their faces. Just heard their voices."

Dale continued to write down what Stephanie was saying. He let Jack handle the questioning. She seemed to be more comforted around him. This gave Dale more time to learn the ropes of being a homicide detective.

"Do you know how many there were?" He asked.

"Two or three at the most. I heard at least three different voices."

Dale kept writing down everything that was being said. "Could you recognize those voices again if you heard them?" Dale asked.

"Yes, I could. I'll never forget those voices."

"Then what happened?" Jack asked.

"They killed him," she said again as tears rolled down her face.

"Killed who?" Dale asked.

"Derek," she said as she wiped the tears off her face.

"Who's Derek?" Jack asked.

"He was my date. We met a few weeks ago at the courthouse. They just killed him right in front of me."

"Does Derek have a last name?" Dale asked.

"Conway. They just stabbed him like he was nothing."

"Where did this happen?" Jack asked.

"The parking garage next to the theater a couple blocks away."

Cappy walked over as he overheard the entire conversation. He was now acting commanding officer. "You two go over to the garage and see what you can find. I'll have Sims and Kennedy look up this Derek Conway."

As much as Jack loved and respected Cappy, he wasn't too thrilled with his first orders as his commanding officer. They were all still feeling the effects of the Badger case. Dale was still pretty sore. Jack's head was still pounding.

"You up for this, kid?" Jack asked Dale.

"I'm with you, partner."

"We're going to go check your story out. You'll be safe here with Cappy," Jack said to Stephanie.

"You're leaving me here with this old man?" she asked.

Jack looked over at Cappy and started laughing. "That's our captain. Trust me when I say this: you're safer here than you would be at the White House."

"We were on the third level," she said as they got up.

"Thank you, Stephanie. You'll be safe," Jack said to her.

They walked out of the bar. Jack wasn't too happy with his orders. All they had to go on was her word. No blood on her. No identity of the suspects or even how many suspects there were to begin with.

Jack and Dale figured they would just walk over. They had been drinking before Stephanie came running into them. They walked through the alley where she had run from. It was dark and couldn't see much. Jack looked around the dumpster and saw bullet holes in the dumpster.

"Look here!" Jack said to Dale.

"Fresh holes?" Dale asked.

Jack felt around the holes on the side of the dumpster. "They're still warm."

So far, Stephanie's story has held up. They didn't reach the garage yet but did find evidence that she was shot at. Jack couldn't tell how many assailants there were.

"I didn't hear any gunshots," Dale said.

"Silencers," Jack replied.

They reached the garage. There were no people out on the streets. It was deserted. They pulled their weapons and slowly walked into the stairwell. Nobody was in the garage. They made their way to the third level of the garage. They aimed their guns in front of them.

"NYPD! If there's anybody here show yourselves *now!*" Jack demanded.

There was no response. They didn't see or hear anybody. They searched the entire garage floor. There was no sign of anything out of the ordinary. There was no dead body or any signs of foul play.

"Look over there," Jack said to Dale.

They walked over to an empty parking spot. There was a puddle on the ground right where a car was parked. It was still wet. Jack called Cappy and Sarah to get the CSU down here immediately.

The Assignment

Within thirty minutes, the entire garage was swarming with NYPD and CSU. Jack and Dale preserved the scene; Cappy even came to the scene. Sarah and her crew were searching the garage for anything that could help.

"It's never a dull moment with you, is it Jack?" Sarah asked.

"Story of my miserable life. What do you have so far?" he asked.

"Nothing much as of now. It will take a few days to analyze that puddle you found. My money is that it was blood and somebody tried to wash it away. I'll know more in a few days. Other than that, don't count on nothing short of a miracle. There is no body, no tracks, or signs of any foul play. The garage has no cameras, so no help there."

Cappy came walking over to them. He wasn't in a good mood. "What do we have?" he asked.

"So far, there is nothing here to suggest that any foul play had occurred. There was a puddle that Sarah took back to the lab to be analyzed. The only thing we do have is we found fresh bullet holes in a dumpster in the alley where our witness came from," Dale informed Cappy.

"I had Jamie close the bar. I sent your witness to the station. Sims and Kennedy are there now working on this Derek Conway guy. Now listen to me carefully. We are still dealing with the fallout of Tackler and Mitchell. Internal Affairs is sending us a new CO, and you can bet your asses they're going to be watching us like hawks. Play by the rules on this one. You guys go home and get a few hours of sleep. You two were drinking, and we are not handing this case over. I want you guys fresh as can be. I'll make sure your witness and secure until you interview her in the morning."

Cappy put his foot down. This was his first case back. After dealing with the badger and the city knowing what had happened, everybody was going to be breathing down their necks before this got started. Jack and Dale knew something was wrong. They went home to get some sleep.

Jack got to the station around seven the next morning. He wore a plain red T-shirt and blue jeans. Dale was at the vending machine by the elevators. He was wearing a suit but with no tie.

"Where's your tie?" Jack asked as they walked into the squad room.

"I ran out of clip on ties."

"You feeling okay?" Jack asked.

"I'll survive."

They went in and sat at their desks. Kennedy and Sims were already at their desks. They've been there all night. They looked like they were up all night, cramming for an exam. They had a pot of coffee brewing over in the corner.

"How was your night?" Dale asked.

"How the fuck do you think it was?" Kennedy replied aggressively.

"Look at the bright side. At least you're on overtime," Jack said sarcastically. "How's our witness doing?"

"She's in Interrogation 1. She's pretty upset," Sims said as she poured some more coffee.

Jack sighed and got up from his desk. He knew he had to go deal with her. He was still exhausted from the badger case. Dale was still sore from his stab wound. He got up and followed Jack down the hallway to the interrogation rooms.

They walked into the side room. They saw Stephanie sitting there. She looked so helpless. She was exhausted. Jack and Dale were standing there, looking through the two-way mirror.

"Have you ever done an interrogation before?" Jack asked.

"This would be my first time," Dale replied.

"She's a murder witness. We'll go in there. But the most important thing is that she doesn't feel like we're ganging up on her. We have to make her feel as safe as she can be but also get the most information that we can."

Dale was as nervous as he was the day he met Jack. He was eager to learn as much as he could. This was his first actual traditional murder case. Dale was up to the challenge.

They walked into the room. Jack and Dale both sat down on the other side of the table across from Stephanie. Jack took out his notebook and pen.

"We just need to make sure we have our facts straight before we proceed," Jack said compassionately.

"I told you everything that happened," Stephanie said with some exhaustion in her voice.

"We went to the garage. There were no signs of foul play," Dale informed Stephanie.

She was so confused. "How can that be?" she asked. "I saw Derek get stabbed."

There was a knock on the door. It was Sims. "Detectives, I need to speak with you right away."

Jack didn't like that at all. He never gets pulled from an interview unless there has been a major break in the case or there is a major roadblock in the case. He was hoping for a break. However, with his luck lately, Jack wasn't holding his breath.

"What is it?" Jack bluntly asked.

Sims handed him a file folder. "This is everything we can find on Derek Conway."

Jack opened the folder. It was empty. There was no information on him. "There's nothing in there," Dale said.

"That's because there is nothing on a Derek Conway. He doesn't exist. Kennedy is trying to go through every database and registry to find anybody fitting Derek's description."

There was no body at the alleged crime scene. No evidence of any foul play. And now no existence of Derek Conway. Who was Stephanie with?

Jack was puzzled. He knew that this was not going to be another ordinary murder case. There was no body to go on. There appears to be no identity of the so-called body that's missing. The only thing they have to go on is Stephanie's word. It was time to investigate.

Dale and Sims had doubts about Stephanie's story. Jack somehow believed her. The fresh bullet holes in the dumpster in the alley from which she came. The frantic fear in her voice. Jack knew she was telling the truth. Somebody had killed the guy she was with, and she was next.

"So what do we do now?" Dale asked.

Jack sighed loudly. He looked through the window at Stephanie. He crossed his arms in silence. He walked back into the interrogation room. "Could you describe Derek to a sketch artist?" he asked.

Dale agreed with Jack. That was a smart idea to do. Jack got back up and left the room again. "Call in a sketch artist," he said to Sims.

"What are you thinking?" Dale discreetly asked.

"I think we are about to step into some more shit again, partner."

Jack had a feeling it was going to be another bad case. Something didn't feel right with him. He always had gut feelings and instincts about these things. Most of the time he was right.

"Hopefully, we can get a composite on this Derek guy and send it to local, state, and federal agencies to see if he's in the system. It's a long shot, but it's all we have to go on right now."

Cappy came walking into the side room. "You guys need to come with me." He didn't seem happy. Jack and Dale both knew that this couldn't be good. They followed him into his office. Sims and Kennedy were both in his office as well.

"What's going on, Pop?" Jack asked.

"I just got a call from the One Police Plaza. The feds want to take over."

Jack hated the feds. They made him feel like he was inferior and couldn't do his job. "Why?" Jack asked. "We have no body, no identity of the victim."

"If there even is a victim," Kennedy said. "You have to admit, her story doesn't make much sense."

"Did the hospital test her blood for alcohol or drugs?" Sims asked.

"It doesn't matter. I believe her," Jack said. "I brought in a sketch artist to have her describe this guy she was with. Hopefully he has a record somewhere in the system."

"And if he doesn't?" Cappy asked.

"Then we play detective," Dale added. Jack looked over at his partner and smiled.

Cappy was getting stressed. He didn't want to hand over anything to the FBI. He didn't even know why they wanted the case to begin with. Was Stephanie more important than everybody thinks?

"I'll hold off the feds for as long as I can. I don't know why they would even want this case or even find out about it. As of now, Stephanie Lambert goes into protective custody. You four will take shifts into watching her."

There were too many questions that needed answered. Kennedy and Sims weren't too thrilled with that idea at all of having to watch a witness. Jack wasn't too objective toward any decisions that Cappy made.

"I'm no damn babysitter, Cappy," Kennedy said to his superior.

"Neither am I," Sims added.

"I don't have any other choice here. We have no body. We have no identity of the body. We have no forensics as of now. We have only one witness. And according to that witness, she saw a murder and she was next. You four detectives are the only ones I trust and are qualified to do. I'll arrange a room at the Sheridan downtown. She'll stay here until we get the composite. Kennedy and Sims will be the first team. Jack and Dale will start their initial investigation. Have we heard anything from forensics?"

"No, we were going to call and ask Sarah if they ever found anything," Jack said to Cappy.

Kennedy and Sims were still flustered that they had to watch a witness. They both weren't usually too defensive about their orders. Jack and Dale weren't happy either. Dale was along for the ride regardless of what was going on. Jack still knew that there had to be something else going on.

Jack went back to the interrogation room. Megan Hollister, the police sketch artist, was in there with Stephanie. Jack watched from the side room. They were in there for a good hour. Megan walked out of the room.

"Did you get a description?" Jack asked.

"Yes. I'm going to print it out and give it to your captain."

They now had a possible description on the victim. Jack was just hoping that this guy that was with Stephanie had a record. Until Sarah called with some good news regarding the forensics, they had nothing to go on.

Dale walked into the side room. "I checked her phone records, nothing out of the ordinary. Mostly work-related calls."

"What are you thinking?" Dale curiously asked.

"I'm thinking that this is going to a shit show. And we're the stars of it."

Safe House

The next morning, Jack and Dale got to the station. They were more exhausted from the Badger case than from the sleep deprivation. Stephanie stayed in the bunk room where other detectives sleep. Jack and Dale went to their desks. Sims and Kennedy were not there yet. Jack walked into Cappy's office.

'What's the word, Pop?"

Cappy was sitting behind his desk. Kennedy and Sims came walking into his office. Cappy handed Kennedy a file folder. "I got you a reservation at the Sheridan."

"Who in the fuck is going to pay for that?" Kennedy asked.

"The city of New York. Your reservation is under Archibald."

"But why the Sheridan?" Sims asked.

"Because nobody would suspect a low-paid social worker hiding in a pricey five-star hotel like the Sheridan, especially being in NYPD custody. It's the perfect cover," Jack said.

"You got that right. Sarah called a little bit ago. She has something to tell you. You and Dale get down to the lab right away," Cappy said to Jack. They both walked out of the office.

"You two are going to take our witness to the Sheridan."

"I'm no babysitter, Cappy," Kennedy defensively said.

Cappy understood how he felt. On his first back as captain, the last thing he wanted to do is make his detectives miserable. This is the only way to ensure their witness was safe until they knew what they were dealing with.

"I understand your frustration. Trust me, I don't like this any more than you do. We don't know what the fuck is going on here.

Until we can prove otherwise, we're treating this as a homicide. She is our only witness as of now, and we need to make sure she is safe. There are only four NYPD detectives I trust with my life, and you two are half of them."

Kennedy and Sims were speechless. They knew Cappy didn't want to make them more miserable or force them to watch somebody. They put themselves in Cappy's shoes. The witness was scared and terrified for her life. Even Kennedy and Sims knew that something had to have happened to her.

"You're right, Cappy," Sims said with remorse.

"It's not about being right. It's about protecting the weak and bringing the killer to justice."

Kennedy and Sims understood what Cappy was saying. They had to protect the witness by any means. They walked out of his office and went to their desks. They got their jackets and walked down to the bunk room.

Stephanie was the only one in there. She was sitting on the bed in a pair of NYPD sweats.

"We're going to take you to the safe house now," Sims said to Stephanie.

"I just can't believe that this is happening to me."

She was frantic and about to cry again. In one night, her life was turned upside down. She couldn't go back to her home or even back to work.

"What am I going to do about work? My caseload is too much for any of my coworkers to handle without me."

Sims sat on the foot end of the bed. She put her hand on Stephanie's leg to comfort her.

"I know it's hard. I can't imagine what you're going through. But you're not alone. You're here with us. Detectives Prescott and Harding are out there right now, trying to find these guys as we speak. You're in good hands. I promise, we will do everything we can to make sure you're safe."

Stephanie was still scared. She did feel safe but still wondered about her safety. She thought to herself, *Why is this happening to me?*

She tried to figure out why these guys wanted to kill her. She also wondered why they killed a guy that had disappeared.

As Kennedy was driving her and Sims to the safe house, Stephanie could not stop thinking about Tyler. He was the only one that made her feel complete. With him and the fact that three guys wanted to killer her, Stephanie was holding it together as best as she could.

They pulled up to the Sheridan. It was a five-star hotel. It looked like a grand palace. Stephanie was amazed on how the NYPD could afford such an elite location. There were bellhops outside helping other guests with their luggage. Most of which was made of pure leather. The richest of the rich stayed here. Stephanie felt like an outcast.

They had the valet take their car as they went inside the main lobby. Kennedy and Sims walked up to the reception desk. "We have a reservation for Archibald," Kennedy told the receptionist.

'Yes, sir. Here it is. Mr. Winston Archibald. Everything seems to be paid for. Here are your keys. You are in room 808."

Sims took the keys and headed for the elevators. Stephanie was trying to put on a brave face. The receptionist was a little suspicious that a woman in NYPD sweats could afford to stay in a room that costs $500 a night, paid for a week.

"You don't look like an Archibald." The receptionist had a sharp British accent. He wasn't used to seeing people that weren't in suits or high-priced clothing.

"Well, you don't look like a hotel that charges $1,000 a night." Kennedy wasn't in the best of moods. They walked toward the elevators.

Stephanie didn't want to be there anymore than Kennedy and Sims did. She never said a word. She just stood there behind them, hoping that this nightmare she was in would end soon.

They got to the eighth floor. It was like a majestic castle. Red carpets going down the hallways. Fancy paintings on the walls. "Here we are," Sims said. Stephanie remained speechless.

They entered the room. Kennedy was impressed with his lodgings. He had never been in a hotel room this luxurious before. The room looked like it was never touched before. It was bigger than Kennedy's entire apartment.

The entry way had marble floors. The furniture looked like something you'd see in a celebrity's house. It even had its own kitchen. Kennedy wasn't minding this babysitting gig after all. Sims looked in the bedrooms. There was a master bedroom and another one next to it.

"You can have the master, and I'll take the one next door."

Sims wanted to make Stephanie as comfortable as possible. She still didn't say anything. She walked into the master room. Nothing was said. She went over and sat on the edge of the bed.

"If you need anything, we'll be right outside here." Sims patted her on the back and walked out of the room. She closed the door behind her and walked over to the couch.

"How is she doing?" Kennedy asked as he sat down on the couch.

"She hasn't said a word. I don't blame her. Hopefully, Jack and Dale have luck finding something out."

Playing Detective

Jack and Dale got to the lab around noon. It was a chilly early-October day. Jack and Dale knew that this was going to be another tough case to investigate. Jack had a couple hunches but didn't want to tell Dale about them yet. Something was off. There was more to this situation that what was put in front of them.

"You are going to love me." Sarah had a smile on her face.

"Well, good afternoon to you too." Jack wasn't in the mood for anything sarcastic. "So do you have anything for us or not?"

Sarah walked over to one of the tables in the lab. Jack and Dale both walked over with her to see what she was talking about.

"We searched every inch of that garage—from trash to used condoms in the stairwell."

Jack wasn't impressed. He was anxious if anything to find something out about this supposed homicide. Dale was not as impatient as Jack, but the suspense was getting to him as well.

"We didn't find anything until we used the illuminator. We used the light to find traces of fluids. And behold, we found blood."

Jack was now into the conversation. Dale was as surprised as Jack was. "How do you know that blood is from our alleged victim?"

Jack was trying not to jump to conclusions on anything. He wanted as many solid facts as they could get.

"There was fresh bleach mixed in with the blood. We were even able to extract a fragment of blood that the killer forgot to wipe. As much as you try to get rid of blood, there is still a chance you don't get it all. Chances are, the blood sample is too degraded from the bleach to get any identification, but here is where you're going to really love me."

Sarah walked over to her computer. Jack and Dale followed. She turned the screen toward them. They were surprised to what they were looking at. It was a partial fingerprint. "Where did you find that?" Dale asked.

"It was next to the blood and bleach. The killer got down on their knees and used their left hand to support them as he or she got down to scrub the blood away. It's just a partial print, so I've been running it through the system all morning."

Jack and Dale were still amazed that they were able to extract not only a blood sample but also a partial fingerprint. Jack loved it. This was his territory. A good old-fashioned homicide. Now they just have to figure out the who and why.

"You guys. Think we may have something."

They walked over to the other side of the table where Sarah was standing. There was a possible match to the partial print that they found at the crime scene.

"It looks like we may have a match," Sarah said in a confident tone.

Both Jack and Dale leaned into the computer screen to see the results. "And our lucky suspect is…Ronald Logan. He did five years in Attica for burglary and aggravated assault. He was released for good behavior three months ago," Dale read off his record.

Jack didn't like it. Something wasn't right. He believed this Logan guy had something to do with the murder. He was obviously there. But going from burglary to homicide just didn't make any sense to him. Why would a guy who just got out of prison risk going back for at least twenty-five years?

"Does he have a known address?" Jack wasn't too thrilled with the result. He had a hunch that Ronald Logan wasn't alone in this. Stephanie did say that two men were chasing and shooting at her. There had to be at least three suspects. He was hoping that they could actually find this Logan guy so he could shed some light on the subject.

"His last known address is a halfway house in the East Village." Dale wrote down the address. They had a lead. It was the first good piece of news they had since they got this case.

"I'll call Cappy and tell them what we found." Sarah was always willing to give a helping hand.

Jack and Dale got to the halfway house around 1:00 PM. It was a dump. Broken shutters and a busted window. They called in for backup. Jack had a bad feeling about this. The place looked empty. Dale even had a bad suspicion about this place.

"Are we going to wait?" Dale asked bluntly.

Jack took out his gun and caulked it. Dale took out his gun too and both got out of their car. They both crouched as they approached the house. Jack took the front door. Dale started to go around the side of the house to the back of the house.

Dale looked through the windows as he was headed toward the back. The inside looked like it wasn't lived in for months. He crouched and moved slowly to the back of the house. Dale grabbed the doorknob and turned it. The back door was unlocked.

Jack looked through the living room window to see if he could see any movement inside the house. There was none. Jack knocked on the front door. There was no answer. He grabbed the front doorknob and turned it. The front door was unlocked too. He quickly opened the door and pointed his gun in front of him.

Dale opened the back door and slowly went inside the house. The kitchen was a mess. There were cockroaches on the kitchen counter. The cupboards were empty. There was no evidence that anybody had been in that house for months.

Jack met with Dale outside of the kitchen. They both went down the hallway toward the bedrooms. The rooms were both empty. Jack and Dale both were bummed that their suspect wasn't nowhere to be found. They put their weapons away and started looking around for any clues that could hopefully help them.

There was nothing much in the house. There was dust on the dressers and mold on the walls. Jack and Dale searched the bedroom thoroughly. Dale noticed something on the floor in the other bedroom. It looked like a stain of some sorts. Jack followed Dale into the next room to see what he found.

"That's blood." Dale was confident about his hunch.

Jack kneeled down to examine the stain. It looked like blood. "Looks like blood to me."

"I just said that." Dale was being more sarcastic than normal. Jack liked it. He was rubbing off on Dale. Jack even smiled at him. He was being more comfortable with him than when they first met.

"It's recent." Dale then kneeled down next to Jack. The blood hadn't completely dried.

"You're right," Dale agreed with Jack's assessment.

"Look there." Jack pointed to the floor.

There was a trail of blood. It was going into the bathroom. They pulled their guns out and walked into the bathroom slowly. The shower curtain was closed. Dale aimed his Glock at the shower, and Jack quickly pulled the curtain open.

There was a dead body in the shower. It was fresh. Couldn't have been there no more than a day. Jack and Dale slowly lowered their guns. They looked closely. Jack was hoping that this was the missing body they were trying to find.

"You think this is our missing Derek Conway?" Dale was hoping it was. If not, then the case just got more complicated.

"I don't think so." Jack seemed confident on his findings.

"What makes you think that?"

Jack pointed to the victim's neck. His throat was slashed. There was nothing about Stephanie's statement claiming the victim's throat was slit. And what's worse is that Jack knew who the victim was.

"This just got more fucking complicated." Jack was now more stressed than normal.

"Who is he?" Dale was confused.

"His name is Keith Warrick. He's a parole officer."

Jack was tired of running into dead ends. Every time there was a lead, it ended up another dead body. Dale was starting to get irritated as well.

"You think he was Logan's parole officer?"

"Definitely!" Jack was confident that they now have a suspect. Ronald Logan was now a suspect not only in the murder of a parole officer but also in the potential murder and attempted murder of Stephanie.

Dale called in the homicide. Jack wanted the scene secured. Bones was on the way. Sarah and the CSI team were en route. Jack got a phone call from Cappy. They needed to get back to the station immediately. Jack knew that that couldn't be good at all. Cappy was never that anxious.

Jack and Dale waited for the team to arrive before going back to the precinct. Sarah and her team arrived first. "What do you have for me now?" she asked.

"It's Keith Warrick," Jack replied.

"The parole officer?"

"He's in the bathroom. Throat slit. Ronald Logan is the prime suspect," Dale added.

"We'll sweep the entire house from top to bottom. I'll let Bones know when he gets here to examine the body. I'll keep you informed."

Jack and Dale walked back to their car. "Why is Cappy so anxious to get us back to the station?" Dale asked.

"I don't know. If it was a good important, he would've told me over the phone."

"So I take it that this is a bad important?" Dale asked.

"Boy, nothing gets by you. You should be a fuckin' detective," Jack replied.

Jack was worried what they were going to walk into. Were they going to be thrown off the case? Did something happen to the witness?

The Feds

Jack and Dale made it back to the precinct. Jack didn't know what to expect anymore. Dale was just along for the ride. Jack wasn't very talkative. Dale knew that meant something bad. Jack's worst fear was that they were going to be taken off the case.

They walked through the squad room. Cappy's door was closed. Jack hesitated to knock on the door. Dale went ahead and knocked. Jack turned and looked at him like he did something wrong.

They walked into the room and saw a guy sitting at the table in a dark blue suit. At first, Jack suspected that he was some hotshot attorney. But he had a feeling that he was no attorney.

"C'mon in and have a seat, gentleman." The guy in the suit acted like he was running things now. Jack wasn't too pleased with him already.

"This is Special Agent Mike Temple of the FBI." Cappy wasn't too thrilled to announce him.

Temple reached his hand out to shake Jack's hand. Jack didn't acknowledge his presence and sat on the opposite side of the table. Dale shook his hand and sat next to Jack. Cappy sat between Jack and Agent Temple.

Cappy and Dale both could see the tension between Jack and Agent Temple. Jack hated the feds, regardless of the case or situation they're involved with. He always felt they could just come in and take over anything and get away with it. Jack had a hunch this was the case again.

"What's this all about?" Jack was blunt and to the point.

"I don't know, kid. Mr. Temple has yet to tell me anything."

"This is nothing personal, gentlemen." He seemed calm and arrogant, like he was about to do something that the NYPD isn't going to like.

Jack's patience was wearing thin. "It's always personal when you people get involved." Jack wasn't afraid to let the federal government know how he thought of them.

"Let's cut the bullshit. What do you want?" Cappy was just as blunt as Jack was.

"I heard that you have a murder on your hands."

Cappy started chuckling at Agent Temple. "It's New York City, Mr. Temple. There's always murder or a robbery or something going on. What do you want?"

Agent Temple smiled. Something wasn't right. Jack never liked the feds, especially when they smiled. "Maybe we can help each other out."

Jack, Dale, and Cappy just looked at one another. "What do you mean?" Cappy was confused as anybody in that office.

"I mean there is more to this than meets the eye."

Jack leaned in against the table. "Well, why don't you tell us?"

"All I can say is that this is bigger than you think. I need to speak to your witness."

"There is no witness," Jack said.

Jack didn't like this at all. How did the FBI know there was a witness? What did the FBI want with this case anyways? Jack didn't want to tell them anything.

"What makes you think there is a witness?" Cappy was playing along with Jack.

Something didn't seem right with this. How did the FBI know about this? What did they want with this case? There was more to this picture than they were seeing. Cappy was trying to stall as much as he could.

There was a lot of heat on the NYPD now. Paul Tackler caused quite a stir. Internal Affairs was breathing down Cappy's neck. Dale was still recovering from his stab wound. Jack was mentally and physically exhausted.

"You still haven't told me what makes this a federal case, Agent Temple," Cappy aggressively said. He didn't like games being played in his office.

"It's on a need-to-know basis." Agent Temple wasn't very talkative. He was avoiding the subject.

"It's our case. We can handle it." Jack wasn't going to roll over and play dead.

There was tension at the table. The FBI just walks into the NYPD and tries to take over a case that the NYPD knew very little about. Agent Temple wasn't too cooperative. It was time for Cappy to play hardball.

"There is no witness. There is no evidence of a federal case. It's a potential murder investigation." Cappy was forward with Agent Temple.

"Where is the body?" Agent Temple wasn't fooled.

There was nothing but silence in that room. Nobody had an answer. Agent Temple sat there with a wise smirk on his face. He knew the NYPD was trying to stall him.

"There was blood at the scene. This is a murder investigation. We are homicide detectives. We can handle this ourselves." Jack wasn't backing off from the feds.

"I can see you are going to want to do this hard way." Agent Temple stood up from his chair. "Good day, gentlemen." He took his briefcase with him and charged out of the office.

"You know, this just got a lot worse, right?" Cappy knew that this case just more complicated. "The FBI knew we had a witness and that she was in our custody."

"That could only mean one thing. We have a rat." Jack wasn't too happy to say that.

Cappy was hesitant to say anything. But that is the only thing that they could come up with. Somebody in the homicide division who is working on this case told the FBI about it. "Not one word of this leaves this room." Cappy was nervous.

"Who the fuck talked?" Jack was irate.

"Who the hell knows?" Cappy said with disgust. "I should've stayed retired."

"Do you think we have a leak?" Dale asked.

Jack and Cappy looked at each other. Cappy put his head down on his desk.

"For fuck's sake!"

"Kid, that is the worst-case scenario," Jack said. "The FBI has unlimited resources and people watching all over the place. If they're involved and wants our witness, then we stepped into a bigger pile of shit than I originally thought."

"We have any leads so far?" Cappy was distraught. Jack could tell that the thought of somebody leaking information from their unit was getting to him.

"There was a mixture of blood and bleach at the crime scene. We're waiting on the results." Jack was just as distraught as Cappy was.

Jack didn't tell Cappy about they had a positive match from the blood results. He didn't want to take a chance that the office was bugged. It was highly unlikely that it wasn't, but lately Jack was being extra cautious.

Dale wasn't as high-strung. He was still new to this. But the thought of one of his colleagues could be a rat. "So what do we do now?" Dale asked.

Jack had an idea. He walked out of the office. He didn't say anything. Dale looked at Cappy. "I think that means go." Dale was picking up on Cappy's sarcasm.

Dale ran out of the office after Jack. He didn't ask Jack what he was up to. He knew what his next move was. "I think I know what you're up to."

Jack looked at Dale while waiting for the elevator. He nodded his head at Dale. "So where is he at?" Dale asked.

They got onto the elevator. "The same place as before. I figured that since you messed up his office that he would relocate. He probably won't be happy to see us. Is he usually there in the middle of the day?" Dale asked.

"No, he has a special hideout during the daylight hours."

Follow the Leader

Dale was confused on where Jack was driving them to. Jack parked the car in front of a big white building. It was the public library.

"What are we doing here?" Dale curiously asked.

"This is his daylight office," Jack replied.

They both got out of the car. Dale was confused on why Eight-Ball would be hanging out at the public library. His character from what he saw before wasn't very silent or knowledgeable that he would be in a place like this.

They walked up the steps through front door. Jack walked past the front desk. Dale just followed Jack. It was like a game of follow-the-leader. They walked through the library. There were people sitting at the tables, reading books, or studying for exams. Dale still wondered why Eight-Ball would be in a place like this.

Jack walked into the ladies' bathroom on the second floor. Eight-Ball was mopping the floor. He was the janitor. Dale was even more surprised to find out that Eight-Ball was the janitor at the public library.

Jack put a wet floor sign in front of the bathroom door and closed it behind them. "How goes it, bro?" Jack said to Eight-Ball.

"Oh, hell fucking no. No way. *No fucking way!* You two white-ass honkies get the fuck outta here." Eight-Ball wasn't happy at all to see Jack or Dale.

"Shhhh, keep your voice down. You're in a fucking library." Jack was very sarcastic to his informant.

"How the fuck you goin' to show your faces here after the last time we spoke?" Eight-Ball was mad and even more scared. He was almost killed the last time he spoke to Jack.

"This is a library, dumbass. Nobody is going to do anything to you here, except maybe give you a swirly."

"What the fuck do you want now?" he aggressively asked.

"What do you know about Ronald Logan?" Jack asked.

Dale was watching door to make sure nobody walked in on their little meeting. Jack didn't have to do anything to intimidate Eight-Ball. He was still scared from the Wall Street station shoot-out. Dale could tell that Eight-Ball was terrified out of his mind.

"I don't know shit." He was being defensive. Dale could tell that he may have known more than what he was telling them.

Jack knew that Eight-Ball was lying. He wasn't in the mood for any of his games. "You really don't want to mess with me today, boy." Jack was not in a good mood.

"Boy? Fuck you!"

Jack drug him into one of the stalls. Dale locked the door behind him so nobody would walk in. "What the fuck are you doin'?" Eight-Ball was struggling with Jack.

He flipped the lid on the toilet. He was going to give him a swirly. It took Dale back to his youth days. He got dunked a lot by bullies in school.

"Either you tell us what we want to know, or I'm dunking your bald-headed ass." Jack was usually playing games, but Dale had a feeling that he wasn't playing. "I'm tired, beat-up, and fed the fuck up with this chasing shit. My partner is sore because he got stabbed by a person I though was my friend. And now the FBI is trying to take this away. I'm seriously not in the goddamn fucking mood." Jack was now irate.

"Okay! Okay!"

Jack dragged Eight-Ball out of the stall and threw him against the sink. "Speak," he said in a low tone. Eight-Ball was trying to catch his breath. Jack took out his gun and caulked it. "It's going to get real loud in here."

"Logan was a piece of shit."

"Tell us something we don't know," Dale added from the door.

"He's in the wind. I want to know where he would go." He pointed his gun at Eight-Ball. Dale was getting nervous. He didn't think Jack was playing around. He was going to shoot his informant. His eyes got big. Jack started to shake. "Five, four, three, two—"

Just as Jack was going to say one, Eight-Ball screamed, "I need time. I have to make a few calls. I'll get you what y'all want."

Jack put his gun away. Dale sighed in relief. Eight-Ball took a few deep breaths heavily. Jack looked down and smirked. Eight-Ball had wet himself. Dale smiled as well. "You have one hour exactly. If I don't get a call from you in sixty minutes, I'm coming back."

"Chill, dawg. I'll make a few calls. I'll get you crack ass what you want."

Jack walked toward the door with Dale. "You need to call a janitor in here and clean up that piss before somebody has an accident."

"Fuck you." Eight-Ball slipped in his own urine. Jack and Dale laughed as they left.

"I thought you were going to shoot him for a minute." Jack didn't say anything to Dale's comment. Dale was nervous again. He could see the strain this was taking on Jack. He was stressed and exhausted.

"What's the plan now?"

Jack didn't say anything. They walked outside of the library and started walking down the steps. Jack stopped and turned at Dale. "You see that black Chevy Caprice parked across the street?"

Dale seemed puzzled. He didn't want to attract any attention. He used his eyes and glanced over Jack's right shoulder. "Yeah, why?"

"I saw them behind us while we were driving here. I didn't see anybody get in or out of the car that I noticed."

"You think we are being followed?"

"Let's go see if Bones had anything on our body."

They got back into their car and started driving to the morgue. Jack kept looking at the rearview mirror on the car. His hunch was right. The same black Chevy Caprice was following them. Was it the feds? Was it the same person who was trying to kill Stephanie? Jack was hesitant to call in backup, but he wanted to see who for sure was following them.

They got to the morgue. The black Caprice slowed down about a half block down the street from them. Jack kept looking in the rear-view mirror at the mysterious car. Dale tried to look in his mirror. They were unable to see who was driving.

Jack and Dale pulled up the morgue. Jack was looking in his mirrors to see if the car was still there. He could see the Caprice parked across the street. They got out of the car and walked into the morgue.

They didn't look back at the car to avoid any suspicion. They walked down to the basement. Bones was in the morgue suite. Keith Warrick was on a slab. Jack and Dale walked over to him.

"You guys look rough," Bones said. "How are you feeling, son?" he asked Dale.

"I'm sore, but still here."

"What do we have?" Jack bluntly asked. He was exhausted and tired of seeing fellow officers being murdered.

"Mr. Keith Warrick. Parole officer. Cause of death, single slash to the throat. No other stab wounds or gunshot wounds seen. I drew blood. Preliminary blood tests came back negative. I sent a tube over to the lab for toxicology findings. My money is that it will be clean. There was some dirt on the bottom of his shoes. It will take a while for it to come back. I don't know how helpful it will be. I did find a piece of metal fragment in the wound. I also sent it to the lab for analysis. Maybe it will help you narrow down your search for the murder weapon."

"Who else knows about this?" Jack asked.

"Just us three for now. Why do you ask?"

"We're being followed. I don't know by who and for what reason. Just don't say anything to anybody. I'm having massive trust issues recently."

Jack was having doubt again on who he could trust. For now, Dale, Sims, Kennedy, Bones, and Cappy were the only ones involved with this case.

"So what's our next move?" Dale asked.

"It's a long shot, but I may know where we could start."

Jack and Dale left the morgue. Jack tried looking out the corner of his eye to see if the same black Chevy Caprice was still there. It was sitting down the street parked. They went to their car. Jack looked in the rearview mirror at the car. He pulled out of the lot and started driving down the street.

Dale looked in his passenger mirror and saw the car following them again. It kept their distance from Jack and Dale as they drove through the city. "So what's our move?" Dale asked.

"We're going to see Stephanie's boss at DCFPS. Nobody just targets a social worker like that. Social workers can make more enemies than cops do. It's a long shot, but maybe one of her cases is the key to this case."

"You think an angry parent wanted revenge?" Dale asked.

"I don't know, kid. Somebody wants her dead. We have to find out who. Whoever it is, is smart. We have to assume Ronald Logan is involved. His blood was at the crime scene. His parole officer was found dead in the last known address of Logan. He is nowhere to be found. Something doesn't add up."

Jack and Dale got to the DCFPS building. The black Caprice was still behind them. It was like game of follow-the-leader. Wherever Jack and Dale went, the car followed. They went inside the building and went to the front desk.

"Can I help you, gentlemen?" asked an older woman sitting on the other side of the desk.

Jack showed her his badge. "Detectives Jack Prescott and Dale Harding. We need to speak with Stephanie Lambert's boss."

"Yes, that would be Todd Markus. He is the division director. He's on the top floor."

"Thank you, Miss," Dale said to the secretary.

Jack and Dale went to the elevator. Jack had a hunch that this had to be linked to one of Stephanie's cases. Dale was thinking the same thing. The only other scenario would be that Stephanie wasn't being honest with them. Jack had a feeling that she was being truthful.

They got off the elevator and walked into where Stephanie worked. There were two other social workers in the room. Jack noticed their desks were more messy and more piled than his ever was. He and Dale couldn't help but feel sorry for them. They walked up to Todd's office door and knocked.

"What do you want?" Markus yelled from the other side of the door.

Jack and Dale turned and looked at each other. They walked into Todd's office. Todd stood up from his chair. "Who the hell are you?" he screamed.

Jack showed him is badge. He didn't say a word. Todd slowly sat back down in his chair. "What can I do for the NYPD?"

"Stephanie Lambert," Dale said to her boss.

"What about her? She didn't show up for work today. So my two remaining members of my staff are working triple hard to maintain their workload, plus her workload."

"She was attacked last night. We need to have access to her cases." Jack didn't want to give details to any civilians.

"Is she okay?" Todd was now curious about his most trusted and reliable employee.

"We can't give any details right now. We think it may have to do with one of her cases. Could we have access to her files?" Dale asked.

"I'm sorry, but those files are confidential. I can't just give you access to people's private and personal matters." Todd was extremely by the book. He wasn't going to just give the police any of his files.

"This is an official police investigation. It would really help us and Ms. Lambert if you cooperate with us." Dale was trying to be as forward and firm as he could.

Jack's phone started to ring. He went over by the door to answer it. "We can get a warrant if we have to." Dale was now intimidating Todd. He wasn't giving in.

"If that is what you have to do, then by all means." He smirked at Dale.

"Thank you for wasting our time, Mr. Markus. We will be in touch," Jack said as they walked out of his office.

"We may have a break. One of the cars that was in the parking garage was reported stolen last week."

They raced to their car and proceeded to the lab where they took the car.

The Stolen Car

Jack and Dale got back to the lab. They had a big garage in the back where they search vehicles for evidence. They couldn't tell if the black Caprice was still following them or not. They went inside and saw Sarah and a few other CSI techs around a car. It was a Mercedes.

"What's going on?" Jack asked.

"We ran the license plates on all the vehicles in the garage. This one came up stolen," Sarah said to Jack.

"So how do we know that this car was involved?" Dale asked.

Jack stood there in silence. He had his arms crossed looking at the car. He didn't know what to think. This case was as frustrating as the Badger case was. "We don't know," Jack said. "But it's the only lead we have right now. You find any prints?"

"We did find a partial print on the passenger-side door handle. It belongs to a Ronald Logan," Sarah said.

Jack never did believe in coincidences. Ronald Logan was involved with trying to kill Stephanie Lambert. Jack wasn't buying all of it though. He knew now for a fact that Ronald Logan was involved with not only the murdering of his parole officer but also for trying to kill a social worker. It didn't add up. There was more to the puzzle.

Dale was holding is right side. He was still in pain. Jack was physically and mentally exhausted. Sarah could tell on both of theirs faces that they weren't at their best.

"Was there anything else?" Dale asked.

"Yes. This vehicle was recently on a dirt road. There was dirt and other fragments in the tires. We sent them to the lab for analysis. It will take a while to finish it. It's a long shot, but maybe the dirt could tell us where the car was exactly. We also found this." Sarah handed Jack a piece of paper.

It was a rental agreement. "Universal Car Rental. That's at the airport," Jack said. The agreement said the car was supposed to be returned three days ago. The company reported it stolen. This was the only lead they had. They had one dead body that is missing. One dead parole officer found in an abandoned halfway house and only one suspect.

"So I take it were going to the airport?" Dale asked.

Jack didn't say a word. He started walking toward the car. Dale followed him. Jack was deep in thought. Dale knew not to bother him. Dale discreetly looked around to see if the black car was near. He couldn't see it. Jack and Dale got into their car and went to the airport.

Jack didn't say a word. Dale was trying to not notice. "How's your side?" Jack finally asked.

"Sore as hell. I'll live though. How are you doing?"

"Tired mostly. Thinking about this mess we're in. Nobody goes after a social worker for no apparent reason. It had to be connected to one of her old cases. Either that or..."

"Or what?" Dale asked.

"Or this Stephanie Lambert isn't being honest with us. And to tell you the truth, I don't like being lied to."

"What's your take on the case? I mean, it seems complicated."

"Well, let's review. A scared social worker almost gets killed by at least three men. Supposedly, these same men stabbed her date and killed him. We have nothing on this guy which means he wasn't who he said he was. We found blood at the crime scene, but chances are it's been destroyed by bleach that the killers used to clean up after themselves. Then we find a print at the crime scene. So we tracked down this suspect only to find his dead parole officer instead. Now we have a stolen car with his print on it. Either this Logan guy isn't the smartest of criminals or maybe somebody is setting him up. We know that he's definitely involved. We just need to find him and whoever else he was with to find the mastermind."

"The mastermind?"

"No way that this Logan guy is the brains behind this. He's too sloppy. Leaving behind fingerprints and being dumb enough to kill his parole officer. I don't buy it. I think somebody hired Logan and other guys to kill Stephanie. We just have to find out who and why."

Jack was convinced that somebody must've hired Ronald Logan to kill Stephanie Lambert. He kept wondering why somebody would target a social worker. Dale was wondering the same thing. Both Jack and Dale were concerned on why a black car was following them.

It was nearly 5:00 PM when Jack and Dale got to the JFK International Airport. All they could here were the loud sounds of the jumbo jets flying low over their heads. They walked through the main terminal and went to the Universal Car Rental station.

They walked up to the counter. Dale was starting to feel sore from his knife wound. A young man with a red vest on walked up to the counter to greet Jack and Dale. "Can I help you, gentlemen?"

Jack and Dale showed the clerk their badges. "Detectives Prescott and Harding, NYPD. We need some information about a car rental from last week," Jack said as he handed the clerk the rental agreement.

The clerk took the agreement and studied it. "Yes, sir. I'll just go get my supervisor." The clerk went into the back. Jack and Dale stood there looking around at the chaos throughout the airport. People were shoving and pushing one another throughout the airport. Dale turned and saw Jack staring at something over the counter.

Dale looked to see what Jack was staring at. Dale smiled. It was security cameras. The clerk came back over to the counter with his supervisor. Before the supervisor could say anything, Jack stopped him. "Do those work?" Jack asked as he pointed to the cameras.

"Yes, of course they work. Who are you?" The supervisor was irate. Jack showed him his badge.

"I need to see the footage of when this agreement took place," Jack said as he pointed to the rental agreement in the supervisor's hand.

"You just can't come in here and start barking orders. How do I even know that's a real badge?" The supervisor was very irate at this point.

"You people gave a car to a killer. I suggest you do as my partner says and gives us the tapes on the day and time that this agreement took place. We can charge you with obstruction of justice. Now please show us the tapes." Dale was more aggressive than usual. Jack was a little surprised himself. He could tell Dale was in pain.

The supervisor went with the clerk to the back again. Dale was holding his side. He didn't look too well. "How are you feeling?" Jack asked.

"I'm fine. Just sore."

"You can go home and rest for a few days. I can handle things," Jack suggested.

"I'M FINE!" Dale yelled.

Jack understood him. Dale was hurting. He respected him even more that he didn't want to go home. Jack was worried that it would affect his work. They couldn't afford any mistakes.

The supervisor came back out with four DVDs. "This is all the footage we have from October 19," the supervisor said.

"Thank you for all your help and patience," Dale said as he took the discs from his hand. Jack smirked. He liked Dale's new attitude.

They walked back to their car. "So what's our next move, Detective?" Jack asked Dale.

"Take these discs and this rental agreement to the lab and see if Sarah can find our man."

Jack didn't say a word. He smiled at his partner as they got into their car.

Room Service

The sun was setting over the city. Kennedy and Sims weren't too happy to be watching over Stephanie. Kennedy was lying on the couch in the living room of the suite. He was going through channels on the TV, trying to find something to watch. He was bored. He was tired of watching witnesses and doing all the paperwork.

Sims was with Stephanie in the master bedroom. She was showing the witness mugshots. It was a long shot, but she was hoping Stephanie could pick out one of her assailants. She wasn't having much luck. They went through three books of mugshots. Sims was getting distraught.

"I'm sorry," Stephanie said with disappointment in her voice.

"It's not your fault. You're doing the best you can." Sims was just as disappointed as Stephanie was. She was hoping Stephanie would at least recognize somebody from the mugshots.

"Do you want something to eat?" Sims asked.

"I don't have any money," Stephanie replied.

"That's the best part about being in protective custody, everything is free."

"The Sheridan has some good burgers."

Stephanie smiled. She was starting to feel better. Sims was too. She knew that it was Stephanie's fault they were in this situation. "Just stay here and relax, and I'll order," Sims said.

She walked out of the bedroom and into the living room. Kennedy was still lying on the couch. He seemed irritated as he was watching TV. "You want some room service?" Sims asked.

"Whatever you're getting," he replied. He just wanted to go home. Kennedy thought about transferring to another unit. All he did was mostly paperwork and helping other detectives.

Sims ordered the food while Kennedy watched TV. Stephanie was sitting on the bed, looking through the mugshots. She was determined to help the police and herself by finding the people trying to kill her.

Thirty minutes went by. Kennedy was getting impatient about getting his food. Sims went back to the bedroom to check on Stephanie. She was getting tired. Sims sat down next to her on the bed. "How are you doing?" she asked.

"I'm trying to keep it together. Every day I wake up and try to think the best-case scenario. I know I'm going to see horrible things. A man beating his wife and children or seeing a mother passed out drunk with her baby screaming in the next room. I've always held it together and have been strong for all those unfortunate people. I try so hard to be brave and strong for them. Now look at me. I can't stop crying and stressing out over this. I've done some bad things in my past, but I tried so hard to make up for it. Why is this happening?"

"I know how you feel. You give so much to others and don't have anything left for yourself. Sometimes you need to take a step back and take care of you first. We're not superheroes. We're human. We make mistakes. We'll get you through this. Jack and Dale are out there trying to track down the people who were after you."

Stephanie smiled with tears rolling down her cheeks. Sims hugged her on the side of the bed in comfort. Kennedy stormed into the bedroom. "I'm going downstairs to see what's taking the food so fucking long," Kennedy said.

He stormed out of the room. Sims shook her head with annoyance. "Don't mind him. He's just mad because he has to do his job," Sims told Stephanie.

"It's okay. I've had to deal with much worse people. I'm going to keep going through these mugshots if that's okay. I feel more confident now that I've talked to you."

Sims smiled at her. "Yeah, that's fine. I'll go out into the living room and wait for the food to arrive."

She walked out the room and closed the door. Stephanie sat in the middle of the bed and went through more photos. She was confident that somebody she recognized was in there. Sims went into the living room and sat down on the couch.

Ten minutes went by. Kennedy wasn't back yet. Sims was hoping he went home. Stephanie was getting tired. She went through four books of mugshots. It was beginning to be pointless for her. She was so stressed and scared she couldn't think straight. She could have seen somebody she knew her while life and not recognize them.

There was a knock at the door. Sims quickly got up and put her hand on her gun. "Who is it?"

"Room service, ma'am," said a voice on the other side of the door.

Sims sighed in relief. "Just a minute," she said back to the voice. She walked back into the bedroom. "The food is finally here," she said to Stephanie.

Stephanie was relieved. Sims went back out to the living room. Stephanie stopped on a page. She recognized one of the mugshots. She couldn't make out where she recognized him from.

Sims went over to the dining room table to get money out of her wallet for a tip. Stephanie was so puzzled on where she knew this guy from. It wasn't one of the guys who tried to kill her. She only saw one of them, and it wasn't him. Then it hit her. Her eyes bugged out of her head, and she quickly got up and ran out to the living room.

Sims was going to the door. She reached to unlock the door when Stephanie ran out of the bedroom. "I recognized somebody," Stephanie said frantically.

"Hold that thought," Sims said as she unlocked the door.

"The receptionist!"

Sims stopped and looked at Stephanie. "Receptionist?" she asked. She paused for a second.

"Get in the bedroom *now*!" Sims demanded. Stephanie ran into the bedroom and locked the door behind her.

Somebody started shooting through the door. Sims quickly jumped and hid behind the front of the couch. She took out her gun and returned fire through the door. Stephanie was hiding in the closet of the bedroom.

Kennedy got off the elevator and drew his gun. He peeked around the corner and saw two masked men shooting through the room where Sims and Stephanie were. "POLICE! PUT YOUR WEAPONS DOWN!"

One of the masked men turned and shot at Kennedy from down the hall. Kennedy then took cover behind the corner. Sims began shooting back at the assailants. Stephanie was sitting in the closet with her head between her knees.

The masked men began shooting at both Kennedy and Sims. They started to make their way down the other end of the hallway. They continued to shoot at Kennedy and Sims.

"THROW YOUR WEAPONS DOWN NOW!" Kennedy screamed down the hall.

"C'mon, forget her. We'll get the kid instead," one of the masked men said as he pulled the other one away. They went down the stairwell.

Kennedy ran into the room to check on Sims and Stephanie. He ran into the room with his gun still drawn. "Sims! Are you okay?"

Sims slowly got up from in front of the couch. "Are they gone?"

"Yeah, they went out the back stairwell. Who the hell was that?" Kennedy aggressively asked.

"I don't know. Where the hell were you at?"

"I went down to see why our food was taking so long. Where's the girl?"

Sims quickly ran into the bedroom to check on Stephanie. "Stephanie!" she screamed.

"I'm here," she said. Sims went to the closet and opened the door. She saw Stephanie sitting on the floor of the closet with her head between her legs.

"Are you okay?" Sims asked.

Stephanie was crying and shaking. "Who was that?"

"I don't know," Sims said. "We have a feeling they were here for you."

Jack and Dale heard the call over the radio and quickly raced to the Sheridan. They pulled up to the front of the hotel. Police cars up and down the street. Jack and Dale saw the CSI van parked in front of the lobby. They thought the worst.

They raced upstairs. Jack and Dale ran off the elevator to the room. They saw the bullet holes on the walls and through the door of the suite. They ran inside and saw Stephanie sitting on the couch. Sims and Kennedy were in the dining room, talking to Sarah and Cappy.

Dale went over to Stephanie by the couch. Jack walked over to Kennedy and Sims. "What the fuck happened?" Jack was irate.

"Don't fucking start with me," Kennedy said to Jack.

"Everybody, just calm down," Cappy said to Jack and Kennedy. "Now what happened?"

"I don't know. I left the room for five minutes and there's two assholes shooting up the place."

"Who were they?" Cappy asked.

"Our murder suspects," Jack said. "They want our witness for some reason."

"What are you thinking?" Sims asked Jack.

"Well, she is either lying to us about something or these guys have a particular interest in her and we have to find out what." Jack just stood there looking over at Stephanie on the couch. He hated not being able to solve a puzzle. They kept hitting dead ends.

"I think we have a bigger problem than that, kids," Cappy sadly said. "Our witness said she recognized the registration clerk down in the lobby from a mugshot. Then two masked men open fire on two of my detectives and escaped."

"How the fuck did they find us?" Kennedy asked.

"We were probably followed," Sims suggested. "How else could they have found us?"

"You think it's a coincidence that a man Stephanie identified from a mugshot just happened to be working at the hotel where a murder witness was staying? Then two masked men started shooting at us? No. Somebody told these guys where we would be hiding the witness."

"Do you know what you're saying?" Cappy asked.

"Yes, we have a rat," Jack said.

Cappy didn't want to hear that. He despised dirty cops, especially with what happened with Paul. Jack didn't want to admit it either. It's the only thing that he could come up with. The clerk had to be in on it.

"Have Sarah go over the security tapes. A camera had to catch them leaving. My money is on the clerk being seen with two masked men leaving the hotel. Check the loading dock cameras first." Jack had a hunch that's how they escaped undetected.

"I'll get right on it," Cappy said.

Jack walked over to the couch. Dale was sitting next to Stephanie. She was a mess. She couldn't stop crying. Jack kneeled down in front of her. He put his hand on her shoulder.

Sims and Kennedy walked over to the couch. They stood behind it and watched Jack comfort the witness. "You know anything about a kid?" Kennedy asked.

"What kid?" Jack asked.

Stephanie stopped crying. She started to hyperventilate. "Are you okay?" Dale asked.

"Tyler!" Stephanie shouted.

"Who is Tyler?" Jack asked.

"He's the kid I rescued the other day from a bad home. I fell in love with him. I don't know. Felt this connection with him. He's the only kid I could think of."

Cappy came walking over to the couch. Stephanie started crying again. "Where is this kid now?" Jack asked.

"St. Catherine's Group Home. They placed him there until they could find him a foster family."

"Jack, you and Dale get over there right away. Bring in this Tyler kid. Kennedy, you and Sims take the witness to the precinct. I'll call the marshals in the meantime."

Jack and Dale quickly ran out of the hotel room. Kennedy and Sims took Stephanie behind them. Cappy stayed behind to secure the crime scene. He had a bad feeling about this case.

St. Catherine's

Tyler didn't say a word ever since he was taken to the group home. The nuns and Father Humphreys tried talking to him. He just sat on his bed, staring at the wall. He was holding the teddy bear that Stephanie bought him tight. It was the only thing that made him feel safe.

Tyler was encouraged to interact with the other children by the nuns. There was no hope. Sister Alexis walked into the room. She was saddened to see Tyler sitting all alone. She walked over to him and sat next to him on the bed.

"Tyler, why aren't you with the other children?"

He didn't answer her. He just sat there holding his teddy bear and rocking back and forth. Sister Alexis was so depressed on how Tyler was responding. She had seen some troubled children come through her home, but never like this. She saw nothing but hopelessness and sadness.

"If you need anything, you can find Father Humphreys in his office. Or if you want to talk to me, you can find me with the other children in the rec room."

Sister Alexis got up from the bed and headed toward the door. Tyler didn't move from his spot. He clinched his bear more tightly. Sister Alexis turned and saw him holding his teddy bear.

"Just remember, Tyler, good things can and will happen for you. You'll see."

He just stared at her before she left the room. Tyler looked down at the teddy bear that Stephanie gave him. He then stared out the window. He thought about what Sister Alexis had told him. He had never seen anything good in his life. If he wasn't being beaten, he was living in fear.

After sitting on his bed for hours, Tyler finally had the courage to get up and go talk to Father Humphreys. He took the teddy bear with him. He went to the door and opened it. He looked down the hallway. It was dark and deserted.

He slowly went down the hallway. The classrooms were dark and empty. He was in no hurry. He didn't even want to talk to anybody. He was so used to being alone. He walked down to the lounging area. There was nobody to be found.

Tyler saw a dim light down the far end of the hall past the lounge. It was Father Humphreys's office. He walked extra slow toward the office. He was scared of just being out of his bed. Tyler only wanted to feel safe and secure. The only thing that was doing that for him was the teddy bear. He had never been given anything like that before.

He could hear voices coming from the office. He walked even slower toward the dim light down the hall. Tyler backed up against the wall as he slowly stepped toward the voices that were getting louder. He peeked around the corner and saw Father Humphreys talking to some other priest.

He couldn't make out what they were talking about. All he could see was Father Humphreys talking to another priest. Father Humphreys looked puzzled on why the other priest was there. Tyler thought it was a bad idea that he came down there.

Father Humphreys got up from his desk and walked to his office window. He saw Tyler at the corner of the hallway. He smiled and waved at him. Tyler smiled back at him waved back.

The priest took out a knife and stuck it in Father Humphreys's back. Tyler was scared out of his mind. Father Humphreys slowly went to the floor. The man took the knife and wiped the blood off it. The killer looked out the office window and saw Tyler standing there.

The killer smiled at him. Tyler ran down hallway. The killer ran after him. Tyler ran into the lounging area and hid behind the counter. The killer slowly made his way to the lounging area. He was quiet as can be. Tyler was clinching his teddy bear.

The killer was searching the entire area. He started kicking the furniture to scare Tyler. "Excuse me!" It was Sister Alexis. The killer hid his knife behind his back.

"Yes, Sister?"

"Have you seen a small blond-haired boy with a teddy bear around here? I can't find him and I'm worried sick about him."

"No, I haven't seen him. Have you tried down the hallway toward Father Humphreys office?"

Sister Alexis looked down the hallway, and before she could say anything, Tyler quickly ran from behind the counter down the hallway. The killer sliced Sister Alexis's throat.

Tyler ran back to the bedroom. He closed and locked the door behind him. He moved one of the kids' trunks in front of the door. The killer walked up to the closed door.

"Tyler? I'm not going to hurt you." The killer knew who he was.

Tyler went to the window. The killer turned the doorknob. "C'mon, buddy, open the door. Somebody wants to meet you," the killer said gently.

Tyler put his bear down and reached for the window. He tried to open it with all his might. It was locked. The killer was driving his shoulder into the door. Tyler reached up and unlocked the window.

"Tyler! It's okay, buddy. NOW OPEN THE GODDAMN FUCKING DOOR!" He started thrusting his shoulder harder and harder into the door.

Tyler finally managed to get the window open. He crawled out the window and ran to the playground. He ran toward the jungle gym. He hid inside the jungle gym. The killer finally busted through the door. There was no sign of Tyler. He ran to the opened window and went out through it.

He took out his knife and slowly searched the dark, empty playground. Tyler was breathing heavily from running. Tyler slowly crawled out of the jungle gym and saw the killer on the other side of the playground. He didn't want to attract his attention.

He lost sight of him in the darkness. He didn't know where he went. Tyler started walking backward toward the fences. A man came up behind Tyler and put his hand over his mouth. "Shhhh," the man said to him. It was Jack. Dale showed Tyler his badge.

"It's okay, buddy. We're the good guys. You're safe now," Dale said to him.

"Get him out of here," Jack said to Dale.

Dale took Tyler out of the playground area to their car and called for backup. Jack drew his gun and slowly walked toward the far end of the playground. There was no sign of the killer.

Jack saw an open window on one of the buildings. He slowly walked over to it with his gun drawn in front of him. He looked around and didn't see anybody around. He went in through the window and the broken door. He went in the hallway and saw nothing. It was deserted.

He slowly went down the hallway with his gun in front of him. He walked to the lounge area and saw Sister Alexis lying on the floor in a pool of her own blood. He went over to her. He checked for a pulse. She was dead.

The janitor came walking around the corner. Jack turned and pointed his gun at him. He quickly put his hands up. "Please don't hurt me," he said in fright.

"NYPD! You see anybody come through here?" Jack asked.

"No, sir. I just got off my lunch break. Dear lord. What happened?" He looked over and saw Alexis lying there motionless.

"Who are you?" Jack asked.

"My name is Henry, sir. I'm the night janitor."

Jack kept his gun out. He was looking in all directions. He didn't want any surprises. "Who is in charge around here?" Jack asked.

"Father Humphreys. His office is down that hallway," Henry said.

"Okay, get out of here."

Henry ran down the hallway in fear. Jack walked down the hallway to Father Humphreys's office. Jack saw the office was door was opened. He slowly walked toward the office with his gun drawn.

He walked in and saw Father Humphreys lying on the floor. He walked over to him There was no pulse. Jack looked around his office. There were no signs of a struggle. Nothing had seemed to be taken. Jack's hunch was right. This kid was a target as well.

Three policemen ran into the office with their guns drawn. Jack showed them his badge. "Detective Prescott, Manhattan Homicide. Seal off this area. Wait for the CSI team to get here."

Cappy got to St. Catherine's about a half hour after the call was made. He was frantic. His first week back as commander of the homicide division had been a mess. He saw Jack talking to a uniformed officer by the back of an ambulance. He raced over to him.

"What happened?" Cappy asked.

"Something is off, Pop. The girl was right. Somebody tried to kill the kid. Killed the father and a nun. He came prepared. Single stab wound to the back and the nun's throat was cut."

"Where is he at now?" Cappy asked.

"He's over by the car with Dale. Why are you here?"

"I heard the call as I was going back to the station. I figured it was you causing shit again, so I came. Plus, we have a name for our hotel clerk that the witness identified. William Barnes, a.k.a. Billy B. He did a stint up in Attica for armed robbery. Was released four months ago." Cappy handed Jack his rap sheet.

"Sounds like Ronald Logan," Jack said.

"Who?" Cappy asked.

"I didn't say anything to you because Temple was in the office and didn't want to take the chance that your office was bugged. We found a suspect from the blood at the crime scene. Ronald Logan did five years in Attica. He was released three months ago."

"You think Barnes and Logan are our guys?" Cappy asked.

"I'd bet my pension on it. We just have to find out why," Jack said as he looked over at Tyler and Dale. "So now what?"

"Take the kid back to the station with the girl. We'll regroup in my office and figure out what to do next," Cappy said.

Cappy got back to his car and left. Jack went over to Dale and Tyler. They got into the car and left as well.

A New Face

It was after ten when Jack and Dale got to the station with Tyler. He didn't say a word during the whole ride. He was terrified. "This is the police station. You're safe here," Dale said as they pulled into the garage.

Tyler sat in the back seat in silence. He held onto his teddy bear for dear life. Jack and Dale got out of the car. Jack opened the back door for Tyler to get out. He didn't move. Jack reached out his hand. "It's okay, buddy. I won't let anything happen to you," Jack said.

Tyler looked up at Jack. He reached out and grabbed Jack's hand. He helped Tyler out of the car. They all walked over to the elevator. "That's a nice bear you have there," Dale said.

"It's nice to have a friend to hold on to," Jack said.

Tyler looked up at Jack after saying that. Jack looked down and smiled at him. They got off the elevator and took Tyler to the bunk room with Stephanie. They walked and saw Stephanie sitting in the corner with Kennedy and Sims. Tyler ran over to her. Stephanie turned and embraced him.

"I'm so sorry I left you," Stephanie said to Tyler as she held him close to her.

He didn't say anything. Jack and Dale watched from the door. Kennedy and Sims went over to them and left. "You don't leave this room unless it's with one of us," Jack said to Stephanie. She shook her head to him. They all left the bunk room and went to the squad room.

They all walked into the squad room. "Cappy wants you all in his office," said a detective as they walked in. Jack knew it was going to be bad. Kennedy thought it was about him leaving his post at the hotel and then getting ambushed.

Jack knocked on Cappy's office door. "Come in," he bluntly said. They walked in and saw a man in a gray suit sitting at the table in Cappy's office. Jack didn't like where this was going.

"What's going on?" Jack asked.

"Have a seat, guys," Cappy said as he went over and sat at the head of the table.

They all sat at the table, wondering what was happening or who the man in the suit was.

"What's going on?" Sims asked.

"This is Lieutenant John Graham. The new commanding officer of Internal Affairs," Cappy said.

They all just stared at him. Not one word was said. Graham had a smug look on his face. Jack was worried about who would take over for Paul. It was the aftermath of what he had done. Jack knew that hard times were coming.

"What do we owe the pleasure?" Cappy asked.

"The infamous Jack Prescott," Graham said as he took out a file folder. "I've been going through your jacket. You're a one hell of a detective. You also had one hell of a month."

"What's this all about?" Dale asked.

"Oh yes, Detective Dale Harding. How's your stomach feeling?"

"I'm fine."

"So, Detective Arnold Kennedy, not a bad record as well. How are you and Detective Sims feeling?"

Kennedy and Sims looked at each other. "We're okay," Kennedy said.

"Where is all this going?" Cappy asked.

"Well, let's see. Within the last six weeks, there has been a serial cop killer running around the streets. Turns out that the killer was the former head of Internal Affairs, who happened to be close to both you and Detective Prescott. Also, it seems that according to the reports and witness statements, Detective Prescott and Harding weren't completely honest with almost getting blown up outside a subway station or disclosing evidence during the investigation."

Jack and Cappy looked at each other. Cappy knew that Graham was going to be a burden. Jack knew that he was going to be trouble with him. He wasn't Paul. He was going to be strict and by the book.

"So what are you getting at?" Jack asked.

"The point is that after the whole Badger mess, the NYPD has been discredited. The entire city knows that the NYPD may be corrupted. Chief Connelly sent me here to clean the house, and that's what I'm going to do, starting with homicide."

"You can dig yourself all the way to China. You won't find any dirt on any of my people," Cappy said.

"Really?" Lieutenant Graham replied. "Well, weren't Detectives Prescott and Harding drinking the other night when your murder witness ran into them?"

"We weren't drunk," Dale said to Graham.

"But you did drink?"

Neither Jack nor Dale answered. Cappy was distraught. Kennedy and Sims didn't say anything. Graham was out to make a point.

"Can your squad handle this case, Captain?"

"What is that supposed to mean?" Cappy asked.

"Well, the last two months hasn't been the best for your detectives. Plus, this is your first case back in a while. Quite frankly, I don't feel comfortable with a group of cops who were at the center of the biggest police corruption case in the city's history."

"My detectives handled that. And they can handle this," Cappy said in an irate tone of voice.

"We can do our job," Jack said.

"I hope so. From this point on, we play by the rules. No more secrets. No more keeping things from your superiors. It stops now," Graham said.

"No offense, Lieutenant Graham, but I don't work for you. And neither do my men," Cappy said.

Graham leaned back in his chair with a smile on his face. "You're right, Captain Pinelli. You don't work for me. But with the recent events that has transpired, I can open an Internal Affairs investigation on you and your entire unit. I can shut you down and turn the witness over to the feds. However, this department doesn't need any more bad publicity. I'm going to give you one chance. The next screwup from any one of your officers, I'll crawl up every one of their orifices with a fucking microscope. Is that understood?"

Cappy was as a loss for words. Jack never saw his mentor like this. He looked defeated. Kennedy and Sims remained silent. They knew they were in a bad situation. Jack looked over at Cappy. He didn't say a word.

Cappy looked up at his detectives and nodded his head. "They'll behave," Cappy calmly said to Graham.

Jack felt disgusted that Cappy said that. Deep down, Jack knew that Cappy had no choice. Paul left a bad trail behind his actions. Jack and the rest of the department were paying for it. Jack didn't like Graham or trusted him one bit. He was a true Internal Affairs officer. He didn't bend or break the rules. As everybody just saw, Graham is here to stay and he meant business.

Graham had a smile on his face. "I'm glad to hear that, Captain." He got up from his seat with his files and headed toward the door. "I trust that you will do the best jobs that you can do. I will be watching you guys very closely. Have a good night."

Graham left Cappy's office. Cappy was distraught. His first case back and he has Internal Affairs breathing down his neck. Jack was disgusted by Graham. He didn't like him at all. Dale, Kennedy, and Sims didn't know what to think Graham.

"Make sure the witnesses are secured for the night," Cappy said. "I'll call the US Marshal's to put them into protective custody. Until then, they'll stay here. You guys go home and get some rest. First thing in the morning, we'll go over all the evidence we have so far. We can't afford any mistakes here."

"I'm going to stay and fill out a report on what happened at the Sheridan," Kennedy said.

Sims looked surprised that Kennedy volunteered. He is always complaining about doing any paperwork. He felt responsible for what happened at the hotel. He put his partner and the witness in harm's way.

"Whatever," Cappy said. "Just make sure it's precise to the letter. We definitely haven't heard the last of Lieutenant Graham. He's probably already ordered for IAB to look into all our jackets. Just tread lightly please."

"Don't worry, Pop. It's nothing we can't handle," Jack said.

Cappy was having doubts. He thought that maybe he should have stayed retired. His first case back had been a cluster. He kept thinking to himself that maybe he doesn't have what it takes anymore. Maybe the homicide division would be better off without him. This case was putting a strain on his confidence.

"Just make sure everybody is here bright and early. We'll go over everything with us at our freshest. Good night," Cappy said.

They all took the hint. Kennedy and Sims got up from the table and walked out. Jack and Dale got up and followed them. Jack turned and looked at Cappy. "Are you okay, Pop?"

"I'll see you in the morning."

Jack was worried about him. He was never this short with him. Jack knew that he was under a lot of stress. A part of him wanted to stay and comfort him. Jack felt like he needed some good company. Another part of him thought it was be best to leave him alone.

Jack left Cappy alone in his office. He didn't want to add any more stress than he already had on his plate. He went over to Kennedy and Sims at their desks. Kennedy was sitting at his desk, working on his reports.

"Are you sure you don't want any help?" Sims asked.

"I'm fine. Just bring me some coffee in the morning when you come in."

Jack, Dale, and Sims left the squad room and headed toward the elevators. Jack was more stressed about this case than the Badger case. Paul caused a mess. The new Internal Affairs commander was harsh and strict. Jack was worried that Cappy was going to be the sacrificial lamb.

Therapy

It was after midnight when Jack got back to Jamie's. She let him stay with her when his apartment got blown up. He was exhausted. Jamie was lying on the couch, watching TV. "How was your day?" she asked.

Jack didn't say anything. He walked into the kitchen and got a beer from the refrigerator. He twisted off the top and walked over to the couch and sat next to Jamie. Jamie knew it couldn't have been that good of a day.

"What's wrong?" Jamie asked. She got up and wrapped her arms around Jack as he sat down next to her.

"We're walking into another shitstorm," Jack replied.

Jamie sat up and brushed her dark hair back to listen. "What's going on?"

"Lieutenant John Graham is what's wrong." He drank his beer and stared at the TV. Was short with Jamie. She scooted closer toward him on the couch.

"Who is he?"

"Paul caused a mess. Chief Connelly brought him in as the new head officer of Internal Affairs. I met him tonight. I don't like him." Jack finished his beer. He got up and went to get another from the kitchen.

"Is he that bad that you're getting drunk?" she asked.

"This is my therapy session. It's a lot cheaper than a shrink. Besides, with being beat up, shot at, and nearly blown up, I think I'm doing pretty fucking well."

Jack had a way of coping with stress. He kept it to himself. Jamie was hoping that he would vent to her. She knew that he has been through a lot over the last couple months. The best thing she could do was be there for him.

"What's the next move?" she asked.

He took another drink from his beer bottle and stared at the TV. "Cappy wants us to play by Graham's rules. We're all going to be investigated. Cappy's under a lot of stress. Kennedy almost got the witness killed. It's just a clusterfuck."

"Is there anything I can do?"

Jack didn't say anything. He just stared into the TV, as if Jamie wasn't even there. He finished his beer and got up and went into the bedroom. Jamie didn't know how to help him. She thought about going after him to comfort him but decided that the best therapy for him was to leave him alone.

Dale got to his place. He was sore as can be. His wound was irritating him. The doctors told him light duty for a month. He never told Jack or even Cappy about the doctors' orders. He didn't want to make anybody think he couldn't handle the job.

He went to his bedroom and took off his gun and shirt. He looked down at the bandage over his wound on his abdomen. He could see blood soaking through the bandage. Dale was exhausted as well. The last couple of months had taken a toll on everybody.

He went into the bathroom and sat on the toilet seat. Dale had to clean his wound every night. He got his antibiotic cream and applied it to his wound. He moaned in pain. It was still hurting bad. Dale had to take it easy but couldn't. There was too much going on.

Dale had tears going down his cheeks. He just wanted to get better and have the pain go away. He re bandaged his wound. Dale didn't want to move without screaming. He slowly got up and opened the medicine cabinet. He grabbed a pill bottle. It was his prescribed Vicodin for his pain.

Dale looked at the bottle for a few minutes. He wasn't thinking clearly. He was in pain and exhausted. Dale took the pill bottle with him into the kitchen. He opened the refrigerator door and grabbed a bottle of Pepsi. He opened the pill bottle and took one pill. Dale stared at the pill bottle and took three more.

He sat the pill bottle on the counter of the kitchen. Dale stood there staring at the bottle. He threw the Pepsi bottle across the room and punched the cupboard.

"FUCK!" he shouted as he leaned against the refrigerator and slid down to the kitchen floor in tears.

*****

Sims went to the Badge. She didn't have anybody to go home to. Usually she would go home and watch TV. But she felt different today. She needed something to take her mind off the day. She was still shaken up from being shot at.

She sat at the bar. "What ya havin'?" asked the bartender.

"A mai tai," Sims said.

She didn't say much. Just sat there, thinking about life. She never really took the time to talk to anybody. She kept to herself. She was lonely.

"There ya go."

"Thanks," she said.

She sat there sipping at her drink. She wondered what was going to happen to her and Kennedy from the shoot-out. At this point, Sims didn't care what happens.

"How are you doing?" said a voice behind Sims. It was her old friend from the academy, Abby Jensen.

"Hey, stranger," Sims said with delight. She turned around and hugged her. Abby sat next to her.

"What ya havin'?"

"The same as her please," Abby said.

Sims was happy to have Abby with her. They used to be close before they got assigned to different bureaus.

"You hear anything about the shooting at the Sheridan?" Abby asked.

"I was there." Sims took a big drink from her glass.

"Oh *wow*! Are you okay?"

71

"I'm fine, just stressed," she said as she took another drink.

Abby caressed Sims's back as she took a drink. "I know a good stress reliever," Abby said.

Sims turned and looked at her. "What?"

Abby took out a $20 bill and put it on the bar. "Let's go!"

Sims didn't know what Abby was talking about. But the way she was feeling, she was down for anything. She was hoping that the shooting range was in her thoughts. They always went to the range after their classes to take their stress out on a paper target.

It was after 1:00 AM when they got back to Abby's place. Sims was wondering what she was up to. She didn't say anything and just went with her. They walked to her apartment. Abby went back into her bedroom and Sims sat on the couch.

She was gone for a few minutes. Sims was wondering where she went. "Abby?" There was no answer. She got up and slowly walked toward the back. Sims unstrapped the safety strap from her sidearm.

Sims slowly walked into the bedroom. It was dark and quiet. "Abby?" Sims said. Again, there was no answer. Abby was hiding behind the door. Sims turned quickly toward her. Abby kissed Sims on the lips.

She didn't know how to react. It was a shock to her. Abby moved away from Sims. "You still stressed?" she asked.

Sims didn't know what to say. "A little bit," Sims replied.

Abby felt embarrassed. She didn't know how Sims would react. Nothing was said. Sims leaned in and kissed Abby on her lips. She wrapped her arms around Abby's back and embraced her.

Abby threw Sims down on her bed. Sims didn't know what to think. Her heart was racing. Abby unzipped her pants. Sims didn't resist. She didn't know what she wanted to happen. But in her mind, it felt right.

Sims looked down and saw Abby taking off her clothes. As she was lying there naked from the waist down, all she could think was that she had never done anything like this before. She lied on her bed, staring at the ceiling.

Sims felt a warm and wet feeling between her legs. She looked down and saw the top of Abby's head. Sims was frozen. She loved what she was feeling. Abby's tongue and lips made her moan loud.

Abby slowly crawled up Sims's naked body and kissed her as she worked her way up to her face. Sims wrapped her legs around Abby's waist and held her close.

Sims threw Abby on her back and started kissing her face. Abby took off her shirt as Sims was kissing down her chest. She took off Abby's pants. Abby felt the same warm, tingling feeling that she gave to Sims. She moaned in ecstasy as Sims made love to her friend.

Sims crawled up to Abby and kissed her on her lips. They wrapped their arms and legs around each other and lied there on her bed.

"You feel better now?" Abby asked.

"I should have this therapy session more often," she replied as they laughed at Sims's sarcastic comment.

*****

It was after 3:00 AM when Kennedy finally finished his paperwork. He took it to Cappy's office. He was sleeping on the cot next to his desk. Kennedy didn't want to wake him and left the papers on his desk. He grabbed his jacket and left the squad room.

He walked out of the squad room and went to the elevators. He stopped before getting on. He turned and walked down the hallway. Kennedy went to check on Stephanie and Tyler. Officer Johansen was standing outside of the bunk room.

"Detective Kennedy, I'm here to check on the witnesses," Kennedy said to Johansen. He showed Johansen his badge. He let Kennedy enter the room. He kept an eye on Kennedy as he walked into the room.

Kennedy slowly walked to the back of the room. He walked lightly to not wake them. He walked over and saw Stephanie and Tyler sleeping. She was holding him from behind as he was hugging his teddy bear that she gave him. He smiled at them. He just wanted to make sure they were okay before he left for the night. Kennedy felt guilty for leaving them at the hotel when they got ambushed.

"You'll be safe with us. I promise," Kennedy whispered. He left the bunk room and the building to get some sleep before the meeting.

By the Book

It was nearly 8:00 AM when Jack got to the precinct. He got off the elevator and went down to check on Stephanie and Tyler. Officer Johansen was still outside the bunk room. Jack showed him his badge. "Detective Prescott, I'm the primary detective. How's the witnesses?"

"You're the second one to check on them," Johansen said.

"Who was the other?"

"Detective Kennedy. He came to check on them around three this morning,"

Jack didn't say anything. He walked into the bunk room to check on the witnesses. He walked to the back of the room. Stephanie and Tyler were still sleeping. Jack didn't want to wake them. He walked back out.

He walked into the squad room. The rest of the squad were staring at Jack as he walked in. After the last couple of months, he should've been used to the stares from his fellow officers. He went into Cappy's office. He was setting up his case board in the corner of his office.

"How are you doing, Pop?"

"Get everything you have on this case in here so we can go over everything," Cappy bluntly said.

Jack went to his desk and got his case files from his side drawer. He then went back into his office. "Here you go," Jack said as he handed his files to Cappy.

Dale came walking into the squad room. He was in pain. He was sweating and his side was hurting. He got the same looks as Jack got when he walked in. He knocked on Cappy's door. "Get in here," Cappy said.

"Where's your files at?" Cappy asked.

"In my desk," Dale said.

"JESUS CHRIST! CAN'T YOU PEOPLE GET IT TOGETHER?" Cappy screamed at Dale.

"Calm down, Pop," Jack said.

Cappy was stressed to the max. He never yelled at his detective before. Lieutenant Graham's emergence to the case had stressed Cappy. It was his first case back, and he didn't want to lose his command again. He didn't want to lose any of his detectives either. It was a hard time for him. Jack understood that.

"Go get your shit, kid."

Dale just looked over at Cappy. He was in too much pain to understand anything. He walked out of his office and went over to his desk. The entire squad room was staring at him again.

Dale looked up and saw Kennedy and Sims walking in. Some of the detectives took their attention off Dale and watched Kennedy and Sims walking in. Sims had two containers of coffee from Starbucks. She took out a cup and handed it to Dale.

"What's going on?" Sims asked.

"Just get your case files and reports and get in Cappy's office before he tears you a new one too," Dale said as he took the coffee cup from Sims.

"Too?" Kennedy asked. "Cappy never yells at his detectives. He thinks of us as his own kids."

"Well, he teared me a new asshole for not having my files ready."

Sims and Kennedy looked at each other. They were concerned. They walked over to their desks. Sims got her files. Kennedy got the coffee and walked to Cappy's office. Dale followed behind them. Jack was sitting at the table, going over his files.

"You have your stuff?" Jack asked.

"Yeah," Kennedy replied. "Got you a coffee," Kennedy said to Cappy.

"Just sit down so we can get this over with," Cappy said.

They all looked at one another. They had never seen Cappy so uptight or irate. They all sat down at the table with their files open. Cappy sat at the head of the table. He grabbed the cup of coffee that Kennedy brought in. He took out a recorder and sat it on the table. He hit the Record button.

"Start from the beginning," Cappy said.

"Stephanie Lambert, social worker. She ran into us outside of the Badge and states she witnessed her date being murdered. The assailants ran after her," Jack said.

"She stated there were at least three assailants. She didn't recognize any of them or wasn't able to positively identify any of them," Dale said.

"We retraced her steps back to where she saw the murder. There were no traces of blood or any bodies at the scene. We secured the scene and called in the CSI team to do a thorough investigation," Jack added.

"We took the witness into protective custody for the night. The next day, we interviewed her. She wasn't able to identify any of her attackers. She told us about her date. She gave us a name, Derek Conway. There was no information on him at all. Our initial guess was it was a fake name," Dale said.

"Sarah and her team found bleach mixed with some blood at the garage where Stephanie saw the murder. She was able to run a partial sample and came up with a match. Ronald Logan did five years in Attica for burglary and aggravated assault and was released on good behavior three months ago. We found his last known address and went to the residence. We found Keith Warrick dead in the bathtub of the house," Jack said.

"We took the witness to the safe house at the Sheridan. Checked in and waited for further instructions and updates. We ordered room service. It was late, so I decided to go down and see what the holdup was," Kennedy said.

"After Detective Kennedy left the room, I went to check on the witness, who was looking through mugshots to see if she could identify any of her attackers. I heard somebody knocking on the door. As I went to see who it was, the witness came out and told me she recognized one of the mugshots. It was the clerk from the main lobby who checked us in. Somebody started shooting though the door. I told Stephanie to hide in the bedroom closet, and I returned fire from behind the couch," Sims said to Cappy.

"I was on my way back up to the room when I heard the gunfire. I took the stairs from the seventh-floor stairwell. I looked around the corner and saw two masked men opening fire with automatic weapons. I shouted at them to stop. They turned and started firing at me. I drew my gun and returned hostile fire at the assailants," Kennedy added.

"After they left, I ran into the bedroom to check on the witness. She was shaken up from the shoot-out. Kennedy came running in to check to see if we were okay. Kennedy called it in and secured the room while I attended to the witness," Sims added.

"While they were dodging bullets, we went to see her boss, Todd Markus. He wasn't too cooperative with us. We asked to see her files for the last six months to see if anything stuck out. He refused to let us even go into the file room," Jack said.

"We then went to the morgue where Dr. Winslow had information about the Warrick murder. He informed us that his throat was slit and had some dirt fragments in the bottoms of his shoes. There was no mud or dirt anywhere near the place where we found him. Maybe if we get an analysis back on it, maybe we could narrow down where he was prior to the halfway house," Dale added.

"We had a tip about a stolen car from the crime scene. Turns out that the car rental place had security cameras. We gave them to Sarah when we got to the Sheridan," Jack said.

"We got the call about the shoot-out at the Sheridan. We got there and was informed on what happened. Detective Sims told us she heard one of the assailants mentioned a kid. Stephanie told us about Tyler. She made it clear to us that he was in mortal danger. We proceeded to the St. Catherine's Home to check on the safety of the kid. When we got there, we discovered that he was, in fact, being targeted as well. We were able to secure him, and I proceeded back into the compound to find the assailant. He was gone," Jack said.

Cappy sat at the table with a blank stare on his face. He turned off the recorder. "I'm going to call the marshals and see about getting them into witness protection. I don't know why the FBI wants in on this, and I don't care. Not my concern now. Kennedy, I want you to go through all of Keith Warrick's files and list of parolees for the last six months and check them out. Sims, stay with Stephanie and Tyler until I get word on what to do with them. Jack, I want you and Dale to check and see if Ronald Logan has any family in the city. He's our prime suspect. I'm going to call the media and get his picture out."

"What about William Barnes?" Dale asked.

"Don't bother," Kennedy added. "He was found dead in the Bronx this morning. Single gunshot to the head."

"Great, another dead fucking end," Jack said.

"Well, let's make sure that we don't hit any more dead ends. Just do your damn jobs," Cappy added.

Jack saw how Cappy wasn't his usual self. Jack didn't want to do anything to get his mentor in any trouble. Everybody was stressed and burned out. Jack respected Cappy's position and was going to obey his orders.

Jack's cell phone started ringing. Jack got up and walked out of Cappy's office to take the call. Kennedy and Sims got up and went out to their desks. Cappy looked at Dale. "Are you okay?" Cappy asked.

Jack came back in before Dale could answer. "We have to go," Jack said. Dale slowly got up and went with Jack.

Dale was holding his side again. Jack could tell he was in pain. "You need a break?" Jack asked.

"Where are we going?" Dale asked.

"Eight-Ball has something for us."

A Good Lead

Jack and Dale walked to the elevators. "I'm going to check on the witnesses before we leave," Jack said to Dale.

Dale didn't say anything. He sat on the bench next to the vending machines. Jack walked down the hallway to the bunk room where Stephanie and Tyler were staying. There was a new guard outside the door. Jack showed him his badge and walked in.

Dale was holding his side and was sweating. He got up and walked into the bathroom. He was breathing heavy and was trying to not vomit all over the place. He went into one of the stalls and tried to catch his breath. He pulled out a pill bottle from his suit jacket pocket. He opened the pill bottle and took three pills.

Jack wasn't the compassionate type. He felt bad for Stephanie and Tyler. He was sleeping in one of the bunks. "How is he doing?" Jack whispered.

Stephanie stared at Tyler the entire time. "He's been through so much," Stephanie replied, with tears rolling down her face. "He deserves so much better."

"We have a few leads. We're going to get these guys and find out why they're after you," Jack said.

"Why us?" Stephanie asked.

"I don't know," Jack replied. "I do know one thing. This is what I do. I solve murders and put the pieces of shit who did it behind bars. I also help people. Right now, my number one priority is to catch the assholes who are after you and protect you at any cost."

Jack got up and went to the door. Stephanie got up and ran over to him. She hugged him. "Thank you so much, Detective."

"Detective Sims will stay with you until we figure what to do with you," Jack said to her. He walked out the door. Stephanie walked back to the bunks and lied down next to Tyler.

Jack walked toward the elevators and met Dale coming out of the bathroom. He didn't look well. "Are you okay, kid?"

"Let's just go see your informant," Dale replied.

Jack was concerned about Dale's health. But he didn't say anything to him or Cappy. There was enough stress on everybody at this point.

Cappy called the US Marshal's office. They got ahold of Marshal Davidson. "Is there any way you could provide witness protection for our witnesses?" Cappy asked.

"Have you identified the suspects?" Davidson asked.

"We have a few leads we're working on as we speak."

"We can't provide protection to witness from unknown people. The purpose is to protect witnesses from people who have the money and advantage to eliminate witnesses after they've testified against them—the mafia, drug lords, to name a few. Find your murder suspects and then we can see what we can do."

"Thanks for your help," Cappy said and hung up. He was more flustered than ever. He stormed out of his office and walked over to Kennedy's desk. He was looking up Keith Warrick's parolees.

"Please tell me you found something," Cappy said to Kennedy.

"So far, six men within the last six months have been paroled to Warrick. One was killed three months ago in a drive-by. Another is back at Riker's. William Barnes was killed last night after leaving the Sheridan."

"So that just leaves three. Call Jack and send him the addresses of those three. Then check the backgrounds on all three of them. Something has to turn up."

*****

Jack and Dale pulled out of the police garage and went to the library to talk to Eight-Ball. Dale was still breathing heavy. Jack tried to ignore his partner's pain. "It's your stomach, isn't it?" Jack asked.

"Don't worry about it," Dale said.

"You're my partner, I'm going to worry about it. If your health is going to affect your job, I'm going to worry. If I cannot count on you to be at your best, I'm going to worry."

"I get it. I'm fine," Dale said.

Jack didn't say anything else to Dale. They shared the remainder of the car trip in silence. Jack didn't want to keep bringing up Dale's condition. Dale didn't want to tell Jack about his condition.

It was nearly noon when they got to the library. Jack looked around to see if he could notice if they were being followed again. There was nothing that Jack could see. He was still paranoid that somebody was still following them.

They went up to the second level of the library to meet with Eight-Ball. They went into the men's room where he was mopping the floors. "Make it quick," Jack said.

"You motherfuckers sure as hell know where to step in the biggest piles of shit, don't ya?" Eight-Ball said as he mopped the floors.

"Just fucking tell us what you want to tell us!" Dale said aggressively.

"Turns out, Mr. Parole Officer Keith Warrick was as dirty as your as your ass on a shitty night."

"What the fuck are you talking about?" Dale asked.

"Somebody was paying him off to recruit."

"Recruit who?" Jack asked.

"Damn, man! Y'all don't know shit, do ya? I should've been a cop," Eight-Ball said. "People who are paroled to him. He recruits them for *business deals* or some shit like dat."

"Recruit for who?" Jack asked.

"I don't know, dawg. Do some detective work. Y'all are detectives, aren't ya?"

Jack just walked out of the bathroom and didn't say a word. Dale walked slowly behind.

"What's the plan now?" Dale asked.

"Need to get a court order to get Warrick's financials. Maybe we can find out who is paying him."

Jack's phone rang. It was Cappy. "You're on speakerphone. We found a few of Warrick's parolees."

"I was doing some digging. Warrick fabricated these guys' records. The parole board aren't allowed to have parolees work or live at the same place. Warrick had all three guys approved for living in the same halfway house in Hell's Kitchen," Kennedy added.

Jack didn't say anything. He hung up the phone and walked out of the bathroom. Dale followed behind him.

"You're welcome. Fuckin' pigs," Eight-Ball said.

Jack and Dale walked out of the library. Dale was holding his side again.

"What do you think?" Dale asked.

"Looks like Keith Warrick was recruiting these guys to go after our witnesses. I think one of those recruits was our murder victim. I bet William Barnes was in on it too. I think Warrick was killed by his recruits as an order from the guy who was paying Warrick to recruit. I just don't know who or why."

The Setup

Jack and Dale arrived at the halfway in Hell's Kitchen. It looked abandoned. "Look familiar?" Jack asked.

"Call for backup?" Dale asked Jack.

Jack looked at the abandoned building. "Go for it. Tell them to come in silent. We don't want to tip them off if anybody's home."

Jack got out of the car while Dale called for backup. Jack slowly walked toward the house. Jack pulled out his gun. Dale took out his pills and took two of them. He got out of the car and up to Jack. Dale pulled his gun. He rubbed his side.

"You okay?" Jack asked.

"I'm fine. How do you want to play this?" Dale asked.

Jack continued to stare at the house. "I'll take the back of the house. You take the front."

Jack walked around the side of the house. Dale looked at the front door. He held his side again. He was in pain. He hoped the pills would help. He walked up to the front door.

Dale knocked. "NYPD!"

There was no answer. Dale reached for the doorknob. The door was unlocked. Dale slowly turned the knob. He opened the door and cautiously walked inside.

Jack walked to the back of the house. There were no signs of anybody being there. Jack was worried that they were going to find another dead body in the house like they did with Keith Warrick.

He got to the back door with his gun aimed at it. He slowly opened the door. The kitchen was empty. Nobody had been there for a while. Jack had his gun aimed in front of him. Dale came in from the living room.

"You have anything?" Jack asked.

"Nothing," Dale replied. "No bodies or any signs of anybody being here."

Jack looked around the kitchen. He looked closely at the microwave. He looked through the window. There was a bomb in the microwave.

"Bomb!" Jack yelled. He pushed Dale through the house. They ran out the door. The house blew up. The explosion threw Jack and Dale to the street. The explosion didn't level the house.

Jack and Dale slowly got up. They were covered in debris. Dale was holding his side again. Jack was coughing from the smoke. He helped Dale up off the ground.

"You okay?" Jack asked.

Dale looked down at his side. It was bleeding again. Dale had an irritated look on his face.

"You good?" Jack asked again.

"I'm fine. What the fuck was that?" Dale asked.

"That was a bomb, dumbass. Somebody used the microwave as a detonator. Somebody set us up big-time."

Jack's ears were ringing from the blast. He was getting tired of being nearly blown up. He looked down the street and saw something. He started to walk down the street.

"What's wrong?" Dale asked.

Jack kept walking slowly. Dale looked more closely and saw what caught Jack's eye. It was a black Chevy Caprice parked down the road. There was one person in the car from what Jack could see. He drew his gun and walked faster.

The car spun its tires as they drove off down the street. Jack aimed his gun to shoot the car. Dale walked up to Jack, still holding his side. "Are you okay?" Dale asked.

Jack didn't say anything. Dale lowered Jack's gun down slowly. Jack took a deep breath. "Go call it in. Get CSU down here."

Dale slowly walked away back to the car. He could already hear the sounds of a fire engine approaching. Jack started to walk back to the car and wait.

Jack and Dale sat in the back of an ambulance while CSU and the fire department worked inside the house. An EMT fixed Dale's bandage. Jack just stared at the house.

"You want anything for the pain?" the EMT asked.

"I'm fine," Dale replied.

Jack got up and walked toward the house. Dale slowly got up and followed his partner to the house. There were firefighters all over the house. The windows were blown out from the explosion. The walls were burnt and charred from the fire.

Sarah and her team were in the kitchen with Chief Wallace from the fire department. Sarah looked at them as they walked in. "Looks like hell spit you two back out, literally."

Jack just gave Sarah a look and didn't say anything back to her. "What do you have so far?" Dale asked.

"It was a minor explosion," Chief Wallace said. "The bomb was in the microwave. As you can see, most of the damage was here in the kitchen."

"You know anything about the bomb?" Jack asked.

"Small, not enough to cause any massive damage. My guess would be a small chunk of C4. Maybe the size of a golf ball or smaller."

"That's not all," Sarah added.

Jack and Dale walked over to the back door. Sarah pointed up in the corner of the ceiling. Jack and Dale both looked in the corner. It was a video camera pointing to the kitchen.

"How do you know it was on?" Dale asked.

"We found part of the camera in the rubble. It had a serial number on it. We checked. The camera was brand-new," Sarah said. "Somebody was watching you."

Jack sighed loudly in annoyance. "Any way to track the feed from the camera?" Jack asked.

"Not really. They probably used a basic video. We'll check into it. The only way to trace them if they used internet access. But I'm not holding my breath for it to be good news," Sarah added.

Jack sighed. "Thanks. Keep me updated," Jack added as he walked out of the house.

Dale saw Jack walking out of the crumbled house. He walked up to Jack. "What's going on?" he asked.

Dale was irate and in pain. He grabbed Jack's shoulder. "What the *fuck* is the problem?"

Jack sighed again. They both went back to their car. Jack got into the car and rubbed his head. Dale got in and grabbed his side in pain.

"Are you going to tell me what is going on?"

"We were set up," Jack said.

"What do you mean, set up?"

"Somebody told our suspects we were coming. One of us is dirty."

"Jesus Christ! Now what do we do?" Dale asked.

"Call the precinct and tell Cappy we have to move the witnesses. Tell him to call the marshals. This shit is getting too serious. Ever since I met you, I've been shot at, concussed, blown up more times than the I care to *fucking* count!"

"What's our next move?" Dale asked.

"Find these fuckers and shove that Chevy Caprice up their asses!"

Taken

Stephanie was going stir-crazy. She was anxious. She just watched Tyler sleep and sleep. He never had much time to sleep in peace without being beaten or yelled at. The only thing that was taking her mind off being killed for unknown reasons was watching him sleep. It made her smile on the inside.

Kennedy and Sims were at their desks. They were trying to find out more about the suspects. "You look tired," Sims said to Kennedy. He didn't say anything back. He was preoccupied with his work. She could tell there was something on his mind.

Cappy came out of his office. "Jack just called. We have to move the witnesses now!"

"What's going on?" Sims asked.

Cappy had Kennedy's attention as well. He was in a deep trance.

"Jack and Dale were almost blown up. Somebody put a bomb in the microwave of the house they were investigating."

"Blown up again? Jesus Christ! Is he trying to go for a record?" Kennedy asked.

"I'm going to call the marshals and try to get them into witness protection. In the meantime, you and Sims get the witnesses ready to move out." Cappy went back into his office to call Davidson.

Kennedy and Sims got up from their desks and went to the bunk room. Kennedy was exhausted. Sims was concerned that her partner wasn't with it. She thought he was responsible for what happened at the hotel. She didn't bring it back up to him.

They showed the uniformed officer at the door their badges. He let them into the bunk room. Stephanie was sitting on Tyler's bed, caressing his forehead. "We're moving you. It's time to go," Kennedy said.

"What's going on?" Stephanie asked.

"No time to discuss it. We're going to get you guys somewhere safe."

Stephanie woke up Tyler. "Time to go, sweetie," she said to him.

They got up and walked with Sims and Kennedy back to the squad room. Stephanie was carrying Tyler as they walked into the room. They sat at Kennedy's desk while they waited for Cappy.

He came out of his office. "I talked to the marshals. You're going to take the witnesses to JFK. They're going to fly them out of the city."

"Out of the city? I can't just leave," Stephanie said to Cappy.

"I'm sorry, Ms. Lambert. Somebody is trying to kill you and the kid. They shot at my officers. Until we know who is trying to kill you, you will be in protective custody with the US Marshal's. They are better equipped with these types of situations."

Stephanie was so distraught. Her life was being turned upside down. Everything she worked hard for was about to go out the window. Cappy was even remorseful of what was happening to her. Kennedy couldn't wait to get back to his old job. Sims was concerned for both her partner and the safety of Stephanie and Tyler.

"Detectives Sims and Kennedy will drive you to the airport. The marshals will transport you to another city and put you into hiding until we find out who is after you."

"As long as you promise to keep Tyler safe."

"I promise," Cappy said.

She got up and gave Cappy a hug. "Thank you so much!"

Cappy smiled at her and went back into his office. Sims patted Tyler on his head. Kennedy went to the bathroom.

"Wait here, I'll be back," Sims said to Stephanie.

She went into Cappy's office. "You have a minute?" she asked him.

"What's wrong?"

"I think after we hand over the witness to the feds, you need to give Arnold some vacation time. He's been up for two days straight, and I think he's feeling guilty over what happened at the Sheridan."

"Kristen, I understand. Jack and Dale haven't slept in days. Dale is still hurt from his stab wound. Jack has been attacked, blown up, and shot at more than a Bruce Willis movie. I'm under a fucking microscope from Internal Affairs over all this bullshit. I just need you to do your jobs, then you can rest. I'm just asking you to please hang in there a while longer."

She could tell Cappy was burned out and stressed to the max. They were all exhausted at this point. She was just concerned for her partner. But now she can see that there is more concern for everybody in the unit.

"I'm sorry, Cappy," she said.

"Don't worry about it. Just get the witnesses to the airport, hand them over to the marshals, and take the rest of the night off. We will start fresh in the morning."

She smiled at him and walked out of his office. Cappy opened up his drawer and pulled out a bottle of scotch with a glass. He poured himself a glass and drank it. He stared at the wall with his awards and commendations. He was wondering if he really wanted to come back.

Sims waked back out to the vending machines, where Stephanie and Tyler were waiting. "Time to go," Sims said.

Stephanie picked up Tyler and walked with Sims to the elevators. Kennedy came out of the bathroom.

"I'm going to go before we leave," Sims said to Kennedy.

He didn't say anything to her. She went into the bathroom while he stood at the vending machines. Stephanie slowly walked over to Kennedy.

"Thank you for everything you've done for us," she said to him. He just stared at the vending machines.

"I didn't mean to put you guys in danger. I let my guard down, and it almost cost you your life. I never even wanted to protect you. I was too busy being a selfish asshole. I'll make sure you are safe."

Stephanie smiled at him. She could see that he didn't care about her or Tyler. She was proven wrong. He didn't see a witness just a charge to babysit. He realized what he saw were two people who were scared for their lives and needed their help.

Sims came out of the bathroom. "Ready to go?" she asked.

"Ready as we'll ever be," Stephanie said. She grabbed Tyler's hand, and they walked over to the elevator. "Thank you," she said to Sims and Kennedy.

Sims and Kennedy looked at each other. "You're welcome," Sims said.

"Anytime," Kennedy added.

They got down to the parking garage. "We'll be at JFK in less than two hours," Sims said.

Stephanie put Tyler in the back seat of the car. She closed the door.

"Do you think we could stop and get him something to eat before we go to the airport? He hasn't had anything good to eat for probably most of his life. He's tired and scared out of his mind. He just needs something he can at least smile at," Stephanie said to Kennedy and Sims.

Kennedy nodded his head. He didn't say a word and just got into the car. "I'll see what I can do," Sims said. Stephanie got into the car. Sims closed the door. Stephanie just held Tyler close to her. Sims got into the car, and they drove out of the garage.

Stephanie was getting anxious as they were driving out of Manhattan. It all seemed like a bad dream that she couldn't wake up from. Tyler was sleeping with his head against the window of the car. Sims and Kennedy didn't say a word. Sims kept looking back at Stephanie and Tyler to make sure they were doing okay.

"Do you think we could stop and get Tyler something to eat?" Stephanie asked.

"I don't see why we couldn't," Sims said as she looked over at Kennedy.

He didn't say anything. He kept driving. Sims looked in the back seat. "Let's stop and get them something to eat," she said.

"Fine!" Kennedy said.

He drove around, trying to find a place to stop. They stopped at an intersection at a stoplight. Kennedy was beginning to be impatient. Stephanie looked over at Tyler. He was still sleeping.

Sims was looking at the stoplight, waiting for it to change. As it turned green, Kennedy started to pull through the intersection. A white van rammed into the car while going through the intersection. Kennedy and Sims never saw it coming. The van drove the car into a light pole.

The van backed away from the wrecked car. Kennedy and Sims both hit their heads from the collision. Stephanie grabbed Tyler and held him. "Are you okay?" she asked. Tyler was shaking from the collision.

Sims woke up. She was holding her head. "Is everybody okay?" Kennedy was starting to wake up. He had a cut on his head. Sims unbuckled her seat belt and reached back to help Stephanie and Tyler.

Three masked men got out of the white van with machine guns and ran to the car. They were the same ones that attacked them at the Sheridan. They opened the back door and pulled Tyler out of the car. Stephanie tried to hold on to him as he was pulled from the car. Another masked man reached in and pulled out Stephanie out of the car by her hair.

The third masked assailant had his gun pointed at Kennedy and Sims as they took the witnesses from the wrecked car. They put them in the back of the van. The third man slowly walked away from the car with his gun still pointed at Kennedy and Sims.

Stephanie and Tyler were screaming as loud as they could. The masked men closed the door so nobody could hear them. Sims unbuckled Kennedy's seat belt. "Can you move?" she asked.

"I think so," Kennedy replied.

Kennedy quickly opened up his car door and drew his gun.

"FREEZE!" Sims yelled. The masked men began shooting at the car. Kennedy shot back at the assailants. Kennedy got shot in the arm and quickly went down. Sims was still woozy from the collision. She slowly got out of the car and aimed her gun at the assailants.

Her eyes got blurry and felt dizzy. The masked men got into the van and drove away. Sims blacked out next to Kennedy.

Amber Alert

Jack and Dale were on their way back to the station when Cappy called. He told them to get to Mercy General right away. Jack and Dale knew that this couldn't be good. "What do you think is going on?" Dale asked.

"I don't know, but from our short history together, I know it can't be good at all," Jack replied.

When Jack and Dale pulled up to the entrance of Mercy General, it was a media circus. It reminded them of the Badger killings. Police cars and media news crews camped outside of the hospital. Jack and Dale knew something was wrong.

Jack and Dale went inside and ran into Chief Connelly. "What's going on, Chief?" Jack asked.

Chief Connelly looked troubled. "We have a serious problem, gentlemen. Follow me."

They followed the chief through the lobby and into the emergency room. They saw Cappy sitting in the waiting room."

"What the hell is going on?" Dale asked. Cappy stood up and walked over to the vending machines.

"We got a serious problem, guys," Cappy said.

"What the fuck is going on?" Jack asked.

"Sims and Kennedy were attacked. The same bastards whose doing this took our witnesses. Kennedy is in surgery. Sims is being evaluated right now."

"How bad is it?" Dale asked.

"Kennedy took one in the shoulder. Sims has a possible concussion."

Jack and Dale were distraught. They couldn't catch a break. Cappy was on the edge. They all were physically and mentally exhausted. Now they have to deal with a kidnapping on top of multiple murders.

"What's our next move?" Jack asked.

"Get every camera within ten blocks of the collision. Try to get a description, license plate number, anything you can. Sarah and her team are on the scene collecting shell casings and trying to get something on these assholes. I'm going to go down and talk to the press. I'm issuing an Amber Alert."

"I'll talk to the mayor. We'll shut the city down, roadblocks, checkpoints the whole nine yards," Chief Connelly added.

"We'll go and get a statement from Sims," Jack said.

"No, you won't." It was Lieutenant Graham walking from the lobby with Agent Temple.

"This can't be good," Cappy said.

"What happened?" Graham asked. "Your detectives couldn't follow a simple task. All they had to do was take the witnesses to JFK. That's it."

"They were fucking ambushed," Jack said.

"Oh, Detective Prescott. Why is it that every time there is trouble, you're somehow involved?" Graham asked. "Literally, the last two months you're the only cop in the city that has been involved with multiple murders, shoot-outs, explosions, and now kidnapping."

"What do you want?" Cappy asked.

"This has become a situation that is beyond your reach," Temple added. "I think it's time to have a little chat."

They all walked out to the ambulance bay. There were two ambulances pulling out of the hospital.

"Cozy!" Dale said.

"I think this is the time to tell you why the FBI is involved," Temple said. "We have reason to believe that Stephanie Lambert was targeted due to one of her cases."

"No shit!" Jack said. "Obviously it has something to do with one of her cases. Nobody hires a group of former inmates to go after, not only a social worker but also a kid." Jack was now irate.

"We can handle this ourselves," Cappy said.

"Oh yes. I've seen what your people can handle," Graham said.

"Until I get the order from the chief of police, we will handle this investigation." Cappy was now irate as well. He wasn't giving up without a fight.

Temple nodded his head. "Okay, Captain. You have forty-eight hours to not only locate your witnesses but also apprehend the people responsible. If you don't, we are taking over. Have a good day, gentlemen."

"Oh, by the way, don't get the urge to go talking to Detectives Sims or Kennedy," Graham added.

They both walked toward the parking lot and left Jack, Dale, and Cappy in the ambulance bay.

"What's the plan?" Jack asked.

Cappy looked so distraught. "Find them. Do whatever you have to do. I'm going out front to make a statement and issue the Amber Alert."

Cappy walked back through the ER. Jack and Dale stood there. They didn't know what to do next. Jack started walking back through the ER. "Where are you going?" Dale asked. Jack didn't say anything.

Dale took out his pills from his pocket. He looked around to see if anybody was nearby. He took two more pills and put the bottle back in his pocket. Dale then slowly walked after Jack.

Cappy walked out of the main lobby entrance with an envelope in his hand to a swarm of news reporters running toward him. Jack and Dale watched from afar as Cappy was getting hounded by the news media.

"Captain! We heard there was a kidnapping involving NYPD officers. Can you comment?" Andrea Bailey from FYNY asked.

There were a swarm of news reporters in front of Cappy. It was the Badger case all over again. He knew that this was going to be another citywide cluster. People from CNN, FOX NEWS, MSNBC, and every local station was there to get their story.

Cappy stood calmly in front of the cameras. Nobody was talking. Everybody was anxious on what he had to say. Jack and Dale stood by the entrance doors, looking on.

"I have a statement. Earlier today, two NYPD detectives were ambushed while transporting two murder witnesses into federal protective custody. Both witnesses were, in fact, abducted."

Cappy took out a photo of both Stephanie and Tyler. He held up the photo in front of the cameras. He was trying to avoid the flashes from all the cameras.

"These are photos of the victims, Stephanie Lambert and Tyler Martin. Their abductors are armed and considered extremely dangerous. There are believed to be at least three assailants, driving an unmarked white van. We are coordinating efforts with both NYPD and the United States Marshal Service. Checkpoints will be placed on every bridge and tunnel in Manhattan. The bus terminals and train stations are on full alert. We will keep everybody informed on this situation as it unfolds. Our main concern is finding Stephanie and Tyler and apprehending their abductors. At this time, we are issuing an Amber Alert for both Stephanie and Tyler. If you have any information on the whereabouts on either Stephanie or Tyler, please call the tip line number at the bottom of your screen. All calls are confidential. Thank you for your time."

Cappy walked back to the hospital as the reporters were hounding him with questions. Jack and Dale were standing there waiting on Cappy. He looked distraught and burned out.

"You okay, Pop?" Jack asked as he patted Cappy on his back.

"Just go find them," Cappy said.

"Whatever it takes?" Jack asked.

"Whatever it takes."

Where Are We?

Stephanie and Tyler were blindfolded and tied up in the back of the van. Tyler was whimpering like a dog. Stephanie was crying, trying to hold it together for them. She couldn't tell which way they were driving. She felt like they were in the back of the van for hours.

One masked assailant was holding his weapon as he watched the hostages. The other two were in the front. Tyler was terrified to death. He was shaking in fear. The assailant reached over and patted his head to comfort him.

"It'll be okay," he whispered to Tyler.

The passenger turned and hit the man in the back with his gun. "Don't talk to them. We have our orders." He turned back around and stared at the road in front of them.

Stephanie tried to listen to their voices to see if she could recognize them. They were whispering too much for her to get a good ID.

The masked man just sat across from Stephanie and Tyler and continued to watch them. He kept looking up in the front of the van to make sure he wasn't being watched.

Stephanie wasn't sure why the kidnappers were telling each other not to talk to them. They apparently weren't acting under their own rules. Somebody else was pulling their strings. But who?

Stephanie leaned over to Tyler and rested her head on his. "It'll be okay. I'm right here with you," she whispered to him. The sound of her voice made Tyler calm down. He didn't cry as much. He eventually stopped shaking and trembling in fear.

Stephanie was trying to recognize any noises that could help figure out where they were. She could feel the van speeding and slowing down. Multiple stops and turns. There was no way to figure out, not only where they were but also what direction they were traveling.

After what felt like hours in the back of the van, it started slowing down again. Stephanie could sense they were about to stop. The road they were on was bumpy. She could tell they were on a back road somewhere. She was hoping they could take the blindfolds off so she could get an idea on where they're being taken.

She knew that the assailants weren't that stupid. She's dealt with enough scum in the city to know a smart criminal from a dumb one. This was no case of lying about beating a child or drugs involved. She knew that she was going to have to use her wits and courage to help them get out of this situation.

The van finally stopped. The assailants got out of the van and walked around and opened the back. One of the assailants grabbed Stephanie and pulled her out of the van. She was kicking and screaming, fighting and trying to get away.

One of the assailants pulled her hair and put a knife to her throat. "Behave, or I will hurt him." She felt the cold blade against her throat. She was breathing heavily.

"Just don't hurt him please," she pleaded with them.

He slowly removed the blade from her neck and backed away. Stephanie started to breath normally again. She knew this was going to be harder than normal to try and escape. She couldn't take that chance with Tyler.

They pulled Tyler out of the van. They walked them into the building. The assailants took off their blindfolds. Stephanie was looking around the building. It was an old abandoned mill of some sorts.

They walked across the old factory to the other side of the building. Stephanie was trying to get an idea on where they were being held. There were no signs or any clues to figure out their location. The assailants made them walk across the courtyard into the next building.

Stephanie looked around as quickly as she could. It looked like an office building that they're being forced into. There was still no signs or clues on where they were. Tyler was crying again with his head down. She walked close to him to try and comfort him.

"It's going to be okay, sweetheart," she said to him.

"SHUT UP AND KEEP MOVING!" one of the masked assailants yelled.

She didn't recognize any of their voices. She tried to remember if it was the same voice she heard the same night of the murder. They walked up five flights of stairs to the top floor of the building.

They walked down the hallway to the last room at the end of the hall. It was a big open office. There was a couch up against the wall in the back of the office. The assailants shoved them onto the couch.

"Behave or die," one of the masked men said.

He pulled out his knife again and walked over to Stephanie. He cut the tape off her. He pulled out a pair of handcuffs and put them on Stephanie's wrists.

They walked out of the office and locked the door behind them. She walked over to the window to see outside. There was nothing but an old abandoned building with woods all around. There was nothing for miles.

She looked around the office, trying to see if there was something she could use to cut the tape off Tyler's wrists. She reached into the desk with her hands cuffed. She quickly looked through the desk and found an old letter opener.

Stephanie walked over to Tyler and cut the tape off his hands. She put the letter opener in her sock and sat next to him. She held him close. "You okay?"

He didn't say anything. His eyes were bloodshot from all the crying he had done. She didn't know how to make it better for him after all that they've been through the last couple of days. She knew there was no way to make up for that.

"I'm going to get us out of here. I'll protect you. It's going to be okay," she said to him. She couldn't make Tyler feel any better, but she could at least reassure him that everything will be fine.

Stephanie kissed Tyler on the cheek and ran back over to the window. She studied her surroundings. They were five floors up. She couldn't climb or jump out the window. All she could see was the old building next to where they were being held. There were woods and trees for miles past the building.

There was no way they could escape from the widow. The only way was to go through the door and sneak past the guys who took them. Stephanie went back over to the desk and went through it some more. She saw an invoice in the top if the desk that said Sampson Paper Mill across the top of the paper.

There was nothing else in the desk. The letter opener was the only weapon she could defend herself against. She wasn't going to take the chance of risking Tyler's life. She walked over to the door. It was locked from the outside. She put her ear up against the door to see if she could hear anything or anybody. There was nothing but silence.

She tried to pick the lock with the letter opener. She could hear somebody coming down the hallway. She quickly put the opener back in her sock and ran to the couch with Tyler. She put her arms around him and held him tight as the door opened.

Two of the masked assailants walked into the room. One stood by the door with his gun. The other had a pizza box.

"What do you want from us?" Stephanie asked.

Neither one of them said anything. He sat the pizza box down on the desk and walked out and locked the door behind them.

Tyler held on tight to Stephanie. "You hungry?" she asked.

Tyler nodded his head yes. She stood up and walked over to the desk. She looked at the box to see if there was an address on it. *Papa Tony's Specialty Pizza* was written across the box. Stephanie was so defeated. She couldn't catch a break. The pizza looked irresistible— square-cut pizza smothered in cheese and pepperoni.

"This is the best pizza I've ever seen," she said with excitement.

She walked the box over to the couch. She put the box in front of him and took a slice for herself. "Mmm! This is delicious!"

Tyler looked over at Stephanie as she was chewing her slice. He reached down into the box and grabbed a slice. He engorged his slice so fast that Stephanie didn't have time to ask him if it was good or not. The fact that he was finally eating made Stephanie relieved.

"Was it good?" she asked.

Tyler nodded his head yes and grabbed another slice. She walked over to the window. "When can we leave?" Tyler asked.

Stephanie tried so hard to not break down and start crying again in front of him. "Soon, sweetie, soon," she replied.

"I'm scared," Tyler said.

"Don't worry, honey, everything will be all right. I promise!"

Needle in a Haystack

Jack was out of options. The clock was ticking. Cappy was under stress. They were short one detective. They were being watched by Internal Affairs. Jack was desperate. He was pacing back and forth in front of the hospital, trying to figure out what to do.

"What's the move?" Dale asked. He was holding his side again.

Jack didn't say anything, just walking back and forth as he always does when he's thinking.

"WHAT THE FUCK DO WE DO NOW?" Dale yelled.

He stopped and turned toward Dale. He reached into his pocket. Jack tossed Dale the keys to the car.

"When Sims is done, meet me at the car. I have something I have to do." He left Dale puzzled. Jack walked around the hospital and saw the FYNY news van parked in the parking lot.

He walked over to the van and knocked on the side door. Andrea Bailey opened the door with a surprised look on her face.

"Detective, what do I owe the pleasure?"

"We need to talk," Jack said very bluntly.

She was puzzled on why Jack was wanting to talk to her. He always tried to avoid her and the entire media like the plague. "What about?" she asked.

"Can I come in?" he asked.

She moved over and let Jack into the back of her van. Her cameraman was in the front seat, eating some potato chips.

"I've always wanted to do it in the back of a van," Andrea said jokingly.

Jack wasn't amused at all. "That exclusive you did with that carjacking ring a few years back, how did you get that intel?"

"I'm a resourceful lady when it comes to determination, just like with those cop killings. You guys think you can solve any case because you have unlimited resources? Sweetie, If I put my mind to it, I could probably find Jimmy Hoffa's body."

"The point is, I'm not one to do this, but I need your help," Jack admitted.

"The almighty Jack Prescott is asking for help? And asking help from me?"

"I don't have time for this shit! I'm having a very bad month. I've been shot at, blown up, and now have a terrified woman and kid out there somewhere scared to death. We have no time. So I'm asking you, please help me"

"What do you need?" Andrea asked.

"We're struggling here. My captain is under too much stress. Internal Affairs is breathing down our necks. One of our detectives is lying in a hospital bed. My partner is still in pain from his stab wound. I'm on the verge of a mental break."

"I'm a news reporter, Detective, not the department shrink. Again, what do you need?"

"We have to find the woman and the kid. They were attacked and drove off in a white van. You think you can work your magic and find a list of white vans in the tristate?"

"*Tristate?* Are you high? Do know how many white vans there is in New York alone? Trying to find a needle in a haystack is an understatement."

"Oh, I thought the high and mighty Andrea Bailey was New York's news media madam."

"How much time do you have?" she asked.

"None."

"How do I get ahold of you?"

Jack handed her one of his cards. "My cell number is on the back. You help me out, I'll give you the exclusive," Jack said.

"Consider it done," Andrea said with a smile on her face.

Jack got out of her van. He didn't like the idea of having a news reporter helping him with an investigation. He was running out of time. There was no time for him and Dale to find the van themselves. He knew Andrea was fast and persistent at what she does.

Dale came out of the hospital entrance with Sims. They saw Jack get out of the news van. Jack walked toward them with a disgusted look on his face.

"Why the hell were you getting out of Andrea Bailey's van?" Sims asked.

"Don't worry about it. I know what I'm doing," Jack said.

"Bullshit! If Cappy finds out you were talking to the press, he's going to blow a gasket. He's already under enough stress as it is," she added.

"I don't know what else to do. We have a murder to investigate, two witnesses to find, and the people responsible for it in less than two days."

"So, again, what to do we do now?" Dale asked.

"We need to start over. Look at the facts of the case one step at a time. Need to start with the lab. Sims, go see if Sarah has anything from Warrick's body. Me and Dale are going to look into Warrick's files to see his list of parolees."

"That's like looking for a needle in a haystack," Sims said.

"What else do we have to go on?" Dale asked. "We know that Warrick was corrupt and some of his parolees are involved. We know Logan is one of his parolees."

"It's better than sitting on our asses, waiting for the girl's and kid's bodies to wash up in the Hudson," Jack added. "Just be careful and make sure you're not followed. After the last few weeks, one of us could be involved."

Sims and Dale looked at each other. "You think one of us is dirty?" Sims asked.

"It's a hunch, okay?" Jack replied.

"That's scary because most of your hunches are always right."

"Let's just find these guys, huh?"

The Parolees

Jack and Dale raced to the parole board office downtown. They both knew it was a long shot of tracking down any more of Keith Warrick's parolees. Jack knew that there was a chance that this was another dead end. He was desperate.

"You need to take it easy with them pills," Jack said.

"I'm fine," Dale replied.

"Kid, I've been doing this a long time. I can assure you, you haven't fooled me. I know you're in pain. Taking a handful of narcotics while on the job definitely isn't helping matters right now."

Dale just sat there in silence. He knew Jack was right and that he needed help. It was a bad time for Jack to address the situation, but it needed said.

"You going to tell Cappy?" Dale asked.

"No, because after this whole fucking mess is over with, you are going to take time off and get some help."

Dale didn't say anything. Jack looked over at Dale and saw the look on his face. He knew he had a problem.

They pulled into the parking garage of the parole board building. Dale grabbed his side as he got out of the car. He was slow at moving. Jack got out of the car and walked over to Dale. Jack reached out his hand to him.

"Give them to me," Jack demanded.

"What?" Dale asked.

"Your pills. Give them to me *now!*"

"You're not my mother," Dale said.

"No, I'm your partner and I'm the guy that can make sure you're busted down to meter maid for the rest of your life."

"I'm fine."

"Give me the pills *now!*"

Dale didn't have the strength for a fight. He reached into his pocket and took out his pill bottle. He looked at the bottle. He was hesitant. Dale slowly handed the bottle over to Jack.

He took the bottle out of Dale's hand and put them in his hoodie pocket. Dale didn't say anything. He just slowly walked away. Jack wasn't happy with taking his medicine away from his partner. He felt it was for his own good. The last thing they need is Dale getting caught taking too many pills.

They walked out of the garage and toward the building. Dale was holding his side. Jack was concerned that he needed be taken off the case. Jack stopped and grabbed Dale's arm on the steps of the building.

"I need to know right now that you can finish this," Jack said.

"What's the plan for getting Warrick's files?" Dale asked. "We don't have a warrant, and I doubt that they're just going to hand them over to us."

"Sometimes when you're in a jam, it helps when you know people," Jack said.

They walked into the building and up to the front desk. There was a young brunette lady sitting behind the desk. "Can I help you?" she asked.

Jack took out his badge. "NYPD, we're looking for Keith Warrick's office," Jack said.

"I'm so sorry, but Mr. Warrick passed away," she said.

"We're aware of this. Our boss called his secretary and told us she had some files for us to help with our investigation," Jack said.

'Yes, sir, his office is on the second floor. His name is on the door."

"Thank you very much," Jack said as they walked toward the elevator.

"So what's the plan when we get up there?" Dale asked.

"There's no plan."

Dale didn't know what Jack was talking about. They couldn't get any files from Warrick's office without a warrant. Dale didn't think Jack would be so desperate to steal them from his office.

They got off the elevator and walked down the hallway to Warrick's office. Jack opened the door and walked in. There was an older woman sitting behind a desk. Dale was nervous. He didn't know how this was going to pan out.

"How are you doing?" Jack asked.

"I'm hanging in there. Is this your new partner?"

"Yes, Detective Harding. Nice to meet you," Dale said.

She reached in her desk and pulled out a stack of files and lied them on the desk. "I made copies of everything, so if somebody else comes looking for these files, they won't suspect nothing," she said.

"I owe you big-time," Jack said.

"You caught my husband's killer, you've done more than I can ask for. Consider this me helping out a friend."

"Take care of yourself," Jack said. He took the files off the desk and walked toward the door.

"Nice to meet you, Detective Harding."

"Nice to meet you, ma'am," Dale said.

They walked back to elevator. Dale was puzzled on what just happened. "What the hell was that all about?" Dale asked.

"What do you mean?" Jack asked. "We needed Keith Warrick's files to see all his parolees and maybe figure out who is behind this mess and we got them. What's the problem?"

"We didn't have a warrant. Who was that?" Dale demanded.

"An old friend. That's all you need to know. Here's a lesson for you, sometimes you need to throw the rule book out the window. In order to beat the bad guys, sometimes you have to get down in the gutter and play dirty with them."

"What do we do now? Track down all his parolees?" Dale asked.

"No shit, dumbass. We start with Ronald Logan and compare all his parolees' release dates and everything in between."

"Do you think all his parolees are involved?" Dale asked.

"No. Most of these guys can't even count to ten, let alone be involved in a murder and kidnapping. But the guys we're looking for are in here. We just have to find them. Let's get to it."

They went back to the car and looked over the files. "Start with Ronald Logan," Jack said.

Dale got out Logan's file. "Ronald Logan, five years in Attica for aggravated assault, released three months ago for good behavior."

"Let's start there. The release dates are a key factor," Jack said.

They looked through the files in the car. "These are the three from Hell's Kitchen," Dale said. He handed the files to Jack.

"Austin Polk, seven years for armed robbery. Was released three months ago. Lennie Jenson, twelve years for kidnapping. Released three months ago."

"I'm detecting a pattern here," Dale said.

"Last but not least, Jeremy Goldstein. Six months for larceny? Released three months ago."

"That doesn't sound like a career criminal," Dale said. "I'm looking though the rest of these files. Nobody else has the same release dates. So where do we go from here?"

"Check and see who visited Goldstein during his incarceration," Jack said.

"Why him?" Dale asked.

"Look at the rest of these jackets. Not one has less than five years except him. Why is that? And look at the charges—armed robbery, kidnapping—and Goldstein has larceny? That's not even a slap on the wrist."

Dale looked through Goldstein's jacket. Jack was waiting anxiously. He was hoping that this could lead to something other than a dead end.

"According to his file, only one person ever came to see him. Miles Dulaney saw Goldstein once a month. Wait a minute. The last four months before being released, Dulaney visited him three times a week."

"I know him. He works in the legal aid office. Why does a defense attorney need to see a client that often? Check the files on Polk and Jenson and see if Dulaney visited them too."

Dale was looking through both files. "Same thing. Dulaney visited them once a month and three times a week for four months prior to their releases."

"Let's go pay a visit to Mr. Dulaney and ask him," Jack said. "Get ahold of Sims and have her do background checks on these guys."

Legal Aid

Jack and Dale raced to the legal aid office. Dulaney was their only link between the possible men that took Stephanie and Tyler. Dale was holding his side again. "You going to make it?" Jack asked.

"I'll be fine," Dale replied. "How are we going to play this?"

"We find him, talk to him, and hope he gives us what we want."

"And if that doesn't work?" Dale asked.

"Then we will have to improvise."

"You really think that an attorney could be in on this? Whatever this is?"

"I don't know, kid. I never thought a cop would be killing other cops and that happened. I never thought a parole officer would be involved with the kidnapping of a social worker and a kid by his own parolees. And that happened. So to answer your question, yes, I think he's involved somehow."

They got to the legal office around 4:00 PM. They were hoping that they made it before the offices closed.

"I don't think he's going to cooperate with us," Dale said.

"Yeah, well, I'm not in a cooperating mood either. For his sake, he better be nice and tell us what we need," Jack added.

They walked into the office, trying to find his office. *Miles Dulaney Rm 207* on the directory in the main lobby. They raced up to the second floor to find his office. Jack opened the door and saw Dulaney sitting behind his desk.

"Can I help you?" he asked. He had on a dark blue suit with salt-and-pepper hair.

"NYPD. We need to ask you a few questions," Dale said, showing his badge to Dulaney.

"About what? You can't just burst through my door and demand answers from me," he stated.

"Do you know an Austin Polk, Lennie Jenson, or a Jeremy Goldstein?" Dale asked.

"I would have to look at my files. I don't know names like that at the top of my head. Why do you ask?"

"It's part of a murder investigation, sir," Dale said.

"Well, unless you have a warrant to search my files, I'm afraid this conversation is over," Dulaney said with confidence.

"Why did you visit these men so many times prior to their release?" Jack asked.

"That falls under attorney-client privilege. And you are?" Dulaney asked as he leaned on his desk.

"Detective Prescott. Answer the question."

"Oh yes. The infamous detective involved with the cop killings. Well, this is a pleasure. I think I may have defended a few people you've arrested. However, unless you want to give me your autograph on a warrant—oh wait, judges sign warrants—and unless you went to law school recently, judging by the way you're dressed, you haven't, so please close the door on your way out."

Jack just stood there in front of his desk. Dulaney sat behind his desk, staring at them. Jack knew he was involved. Dulaney wasn't going to make this easy for them.

"Thank you for your time, asswipe," Jack said as he walked out the door.

"Anything I can do to help the NYPD," Dulaney said with a smile on his face.

Dale walked up to Jack as he was walking down the steps. "Well, that was cooperative," Dale said.

"Yeah, I saw that coming. So now we play dirty."

"You're going to break into his office? That's a little intense, even for you."

"Jesus Christ, I need a vacation! We're going to follow him, moron."

"What good will that do?" Dale asked. "I don't think he's dumb enough to go to where Stephanie and Tyler are being held."

"We rattled the rat's cage. We confronted him about his clients. He denies it. He'll panic, and we wait for him to make a mistake. He's involved in this. Just can't figure out what this is all about. That's where we come in."

Jack and Dale went back to their car to wait for Dulaney. He came walking out of the office about fifteen minutes later. "There he is," Dale said.

He hailed a cab and got into the back seat. Jack put the car into Drive and started following the taxi. He maintained a distance from the cab to make sure they weren't being spotted by Dulaney.

"What do you think this means?" Dale asked.

"I don't know, kid. I'm starting to get worried on how far this is taking us. First, a parole officer and now a defense attorney. Just worried to see where the next bread crumb on the trail will lead us to."

The taxi stopped at a café in Midtown. Jack pulled over away behind the cab. Dulaney got out and went inside the café.

"Let's go and see what he's doing," Dale said as he opened his car door.

Jack stopped him. "Wait!"

"What's going on?" Dale asked.

"Look, the cab isn't leaving. My guess that he's making a phone call. We wait."

Dulaney came out of the café about five minutes later. He leaned in the passenger side of the cab and paid the driver. He ran across the street through traffic. He got into another taxi and drove off.

Jack tried to turn around and follow him. There were too many cars coming from the opposite side of the street. They lost him.

"Fuck!" Jack screamed.

"Now what?" Dale asked.

Jack's cell phone was ringing. "Yeah," he said. "Perfect. Thanks, Sims."

"What was that all about?" Dale asked.

"That was Kristen. It seems Jeremy Goldstein has a mother that lives just four blocks from here."

"Let's go pay her a visit," Dale said.

A Mother's Tale

Jack and Dale got to the address in Midtown where Goldstein's mother lives. It was an old apartment building for needy families.

"The projects of Midtown," Jack said. "At least one homicide a week, multiple drive-by shootings. Be thankful for what you have."

They got out and walked across the courtyard of the building. Young teenagers were playing basketball on the asphalt. An old man in a wheelchair was feeding the birds by the front door. They could hear rap music playing from an apartment from afar.

They walked in the doorway and walked down the hallway to room 1F. Jack knocked on the door. Dale leaned in and could hear the TV on. "Somebody is home," Dale said.

Jack knocked on the door again. "NYPD! Open up," yelled Jack. Dale knocked on the door as well. The door finally opened. It was a middle-aged-looking woman with purple pajamas on holding a cigarette.

"Mrs. Goldstein?" Dale asked.

"What did he do now?" she asked.

"Detectives Prescott and Harding. He?" Jack asked.

"The only time the police are here is when my Jeremy is in trouble. So I figured he must've done something dumb again."

"Well, it is urgent that we try to find him," Jack said. "May we come in and ask you a few questions?"

"If you must," she replied as she coughed from her cigarette. "Don't mind the place. I wasn't expecting company."

Jack and Dale looked around the apartment as they were walking in. Pizza boxes on the floor, clothes all over the place. The entire room smelled like menthols. Dale was coughing, trying to hide it.

"We looked at your son's prison records. We were just wondering what kind of person Jeremy is," Jack wondered.

Mrs. Goldstein sat down in her recliner in the living room. She put out her cigarette and lit another. Jack and Dale sat on the couch in front of her. Dale had to move some clothes out of the way before he could sit down.

"It saddens me," Mrs. Goldstein said. "He was always such a good boy."

"What happened?" Dale asked.

"Jeremy's father died when he was thirteen. He had no life insurance to help support us. I had to move down to part-time to watch Jeremy. He tried so hard to help make extra money for us. I warned him over and over again to concentrate on school and make a better life for himself. He wouldn't accept that. He tried too hard to make money. He would walk dogs, help old ladies with their groceries. That wasn't enough."

"What went wrong?" Jack asked.

"About two years ago, Jeremy was out of high school and tried to get an actual job. Nobody would hire white ghetto trash, as he put it. So he got himself some friends that would take things instead of earning them."

"Is that how he got arrested?" Dale asked.

"Yeah," Mrs. Goldstein replied as she inhaled her cigarette. "His *friends* threw him under the bus. They pleaded down to a misdemeanor charge. He got six months inside."

"According to his file, you didn't go see him while he was incarcerated. Why is that?" Jack asked.

"I couldn't go and see him locked up like a caged animal for trying to help me out. I'm so ashamed that I couldn't provide him with a better life. As a mother, you try to make a better life for your kids. I failed. He was so determined to help me when I should've helped him. I couldn't even have the courage to go see him and tell him I was sorry."

Dale was holding his side again. He was starting to get sweaty. Jack was noticing the pain he was in. Mrs. Goldstein started crying as she smoked her cigarette.

"Are you okay, Detective?" she asked Dale.

Dale tried to avoid her obvious concern for him. "Did Jeremy come see you when he got out?" Dale asked.

"He came to see me about two months ago. He was excited. He told me that his lawyer got him a new job that paid big money. I was worried he was getting into trouble again. I begged him to focus on life and go to college and make something of himself. He kept going on and on about how this could be his chance to make some real money and get us a better life. That's all he told me. He said I love you and left. I haven't heard from him since. He also said he told his old friend, Danny O'Malley, who lives down the hallway in 1P about it as well. Maybe he could tell you more."

She wiped the tears from her face. Dale wiped the sweat from his forehead. Jack started to get a headache. He rubbed his temples.

"Did Jeremy say where he was staying?" Jack asked.

"No, he just said he loved me and would be back when the job was done. I just wished I could've done more to be a better mother. It didn't have to be this way."

She started crying again. Jack got up and went over to her. He patted her on her back. "It'll be okay," Jack said.

"Thank you for your time," Dale said as he slowly got up.

Jack and Dale walked to the front door. "WAIT!" Mrs. Goldstein shouted. "I may be stupid with my life choices, but I'm not dumb. How much trouble is he in?"

Jack and Dale looked at each other. They were hesitant to say anything to her. "We think Jeremy may be involved with a kidnapping and murder," Jack said.

Mrs. Goldstein started shaking and crying even more. Dale didn't agree with Jack telling her the truth about her son. She looked to be in rough shape as it is. Jack left the apartment and walked down the hallway.

Dale stood there staring at Mrs. Goldstein. He felt like he should've said something. "I'll do what I can to bring him in alive," Dale said.

"Thank you so much."

Dale just walked out the door and followed Jack down the hallway. "Why the hell did you tell her son may be involved in a kidnapping and murder?"

Jack just ignored Dale and kept walking. "Hey!" Dale said as he stopped. Jack stopped and turned to face him. He walked toward Dale.

"She already knew something was wrong when we showed up. I wasn't going to let her sit on pins and needles, worrying every minute."

"So you tell her and then what? You don't think she is going to worry more now?" Dale asked.

"And you telling her that you will bring her son home alive? Don't make promises you won't be able to keep, kid," Jack said. "Let's go see this friend of Goldstein's. Hopefully he has something more than what Mom had."

Jack and Dale walked down the hallway. "It's 1P," Jack said. Dale knocked on the door. A young guy in a torn T-shirt answered the door.

"What do you want?" he bluntly asked.

Dale showed him his badge. "NYPD. Are you Danny O'Malley?"

"I didn't do shit. Whatever they said I did, I didn't," O'Malley said.

"We're here to ask you about Jeremy Goldstein," Jack said."

"Oh, what about him? Is he okay?" Danny asked.

Dale started holding his side again and turned away. Jack stood in between him and O'Malley. "We need to find him. His mother told us he talked to you when he got out of prison three months ago. What did you and Jeremy talk about?"

"What's it to you?" Danny said. He was being very defensive. Jack and Dale didn't have time or patience to deal with anything.

"I'm not going to lie to you, Danny. I am not in the mood to play games," Jack said. "All I want to know is what Jeremy talked to you about when he got out of prison."

"I don't have to say anything to you, pigs. Now get the hell out of here," O'Malley said.

Dale pushed Jack out of the way and shoved O'Malley up against the wall.

"What the fuck is wrong with you?" O'Malley yelled.

Dale pulled out his gun and pointed it at his head.

"What the hell is wrong with you, kid?" Jack asked

Dale didn't say anything. He just stared at O'Malley's face. "C'mon, kid, you need to calm down."

Jack was trying to be persistent. Dale had snapped. He was in pain and hadn't slept in days. Jack was regretting taking his pills away from him. He was worried that Dale had reached his breaking point.

"What did Jeremy talk to you about?" Dale asked.

"Go fuck yourself!" O'Malley shouted.

Dale quickly turned the gun away and fired it by his head.

"Jesus Christ! You're fucking insane!" O'Malley yelled.

"What the hell is wrong with you, kid?" Jack asked.

"The next one will kill you," Dale said as he pointed the gun back at O'Malley's head. Dale wasn't bluffing. Jack was scared that Dale lost it.

"You need to calm down, Dale," Jack said. He stood beside him, trying to reason with him. "This is about to go bad for you."

"You need to tell us what we need to know before you're able to whistle through your forehead," Dale said. He caulked his gun and aimed it back at O'Malley's head.

"Wait! Stop! You're fucking insane."

"We'll commit him later. I think this would be the time to start speaking," Jack said.

Dale lowered his gun slowly. Jack and O'Malley sighed with relief. Jack was uncertain if Dale was really going to pull the trigger. Dale was in pain and agony. He wasn't in the right state of mind.

"Speak," Dale said.

"Jeremy came to see me about three months ago. He was all frantic about getting this well-paying job."

"What was the job?" Dale asked.

"He never said. All he talked about what his lawyer got him this *gig* that pays well. I asked Jeremy what this gig was. He didn't even know. All he said was his lawyer got him and a few other inmates a gig that pays well. All he wanted to do was make his mom proud of him. I said this wasn't the way to do it. He didn't like that and told me never mind. That was the last time I saw him."

"Are you sure he said his lawyer?" Jack asked.

"Yeah. That's what made me say no. It sounded too shady. I may me a lot of things, but I earn what I make. It didn't sound right. I tried to talk Jeremy out of it. But he was determined."

"Thanks for your time," Jack said. Dale put his gun back in its holster.

"I'm sorry I scared you," Dale said.

Dale and Jack walked down the hallway.

"Hey, if you find Jeremy, be easy on him. He's had it rough," O'Malley said.

"I won't make any promises," Dale said.

"Why didn't you promise him?" Jack asked.

Dale didn't say anything. He just kept walking down the hall-way. Jack was now getting a taste of his own medicine.

"How's your side?" Jack asked as they walked outside.

Dale just kept walking. He didn't say anything to Jack. "Hey!"

Dale stopped in the middle of the courtyard. "It's getting worse," Dale admitted.

Jack sighed. He didn't want to make Dale feel worse. He reached into his pocket and pulled out Dale's pill bottle. Dale looked like a dog waiting for a treat. Jack opened the bottle and poured a pill into his hand.

"Here," Jack said as he extended his hand out to Dale.

Dale just stared at his hand. He was resistant on taking it. Jack could tell he was in pain. He wasn't thinking clearly. Jack needed him more than he let on. Dale reached out and took the pill.

"I'm sorry," Dale said.

"You'll get through this, kid."

Dale was about to put the pill into his mouth. He stopped and stared across the side street. "What's your problem now?" Jack asked.

"It's here," Dale said.

Jack turned around to see what Dale was talking about. It was the black Chevy Caprice. It followed them again. "Can you see anybody inside?" Jack asked.

"No. Let's surprise them."

"I'll take this side. You go around and cover the back," Jack said to Dale.

Dale held his side as he walked around the apartment complex. Jack tried to be discreet as he walked around the basketball court. Jack reached under his hoodie to grab his gun. Dale took out his gun. He ducked down as he approached the back of the car. Jack ran across the street to the car.

They both went to the driver's side with the guns drawn. There was nobody in the car.

"Where the hell is he?" Dale asked.

"He's around here somewhere," Jack said. He looked around to see if he could spot anybody out of the ordinary.

A gunshot came from the apartment complex. Jack and Dale looked at each other. They thought the worst. They drew their guns and ran back toward the complex. The kids on the basketball court were running toward the building.

"NYPD! STAY BACK!" Jack yelled.

Jack leaned against the wall and slowly walked down the hallway. Dale leaned across the other wall. O'Malley's door was open. Jack kicked the door open and saw O'Malley lying there in a pool of his own blood. He had been shot in the chest. Jack leaned down to check for a pulse. O'Malley was dead.

"The car," Jack said.

He ran down the hallway, out the door. Dale followed. Jack and Dale ran across the courtyard to other side of the complex. The black Chevy Caprice sped away down the street. Jack and Dale lost their killer.

It'll Be Okay

Stephanie was sitting on the couch with Tyler. She could see the sun setting out the window. Tyler had finally gone back to sleep. She kept going through her mind why this was happening to them. She tried to think of all the cases she had been involved with.

She could hear somebody walking down the hallway toward the office. Stephanie clinched her hands as the footsteps got closer to the door. The door opened. Two of the masked men came into the office.

"Please don't wake him," Stephanie whispered.

One of the masked men threw a blanket at her. They didn't say anything. They looked around the room and walked back out. Stephanie took the blanket and covered herself and Tyler with it. She couldn't risk putting Tyler in anymore danger. But she had to try and find a way out of there.

There was nothing she could do now. The best thing she could do is try to rest. She leaned her arm on the armrest of the couch. It was the first time in days she felt relaxed. Both Stephanie and Tyler were sound asleep.

It was after midnight. The office door opened slowly. It was one of the masked men. He slowly walked toward the couch. He stood over Stephanie and leaned down. Stephanie opened her eyes and was about to scream. The masked man quickly put his hand over her mouth.

"Calm down. I'm not going to hurt you," he whispered.

Stephanie was squirming and trying to break free. "You don't want to wake Tyler, do you?" he asked.

She stopped resisting. She had no choice. He slowly removed his hand from her mouth. She just sat there, looking up at this dark figure standing over her.

He leaned on one knee next to the couch. He took his mask off in front of her. Stephanie was confused.

"My name is Jeremy. I'm so sorry about all this," he whispered.

"What the hell is going on? Why do you people want us?"

"To tell you the truth, I don't know. I didn't sign up for this."

"Sign up for what?" Stephanie asked.

"I don't know, man. All I know is I needed money for my mom, and the next thing I know, I'm shooting at police in a hotel and kidnapping you and that kid. I asked what was going on, and nobody is telling me nothing. I can't do this anymore. I just wanted to tell you that I'm sorry and that it'll be okay."

For some reason, Stephanie trusted Jeremy. She dealt with scum her whole life. She can tell when people are lying or telling the truth. She looked down at Tyler sleeping on her lap.

"How do we get out of here?" she asked.

Jeremy looked to make sure nobody else was around. "We're on the fifth floor. There is a stairwell at the end of the hallway. Take the stairs down to the basement. You and the kid run down the road to the main highway."

"How do we get past your *friends?*"

"I'll make a distraction. When I do, you have to move quick."

Stephanie wasn't sure about this. A part of her wanted to just stay put and wait for Jack and Dale to rescue them. Another part was thinking she had to get Tyler to safety. She had no choice but to trust him.

Jeremy handed Stephanie a small flashlight. "Take this. You'll need it."

Stephanie took the flashlight and looked down at Tyler. "Thank you," she whispered.

"Don't thank me. I'm trying to make things right for all the fucked-up things I've done. Just get that kid out of here. I'll take care of the rest."

"What about you?" Stephanie asked.

"When you make it through this, could you give this to my mom?" Jeremy handed Stephanie a letter. "It's got her address on it. You don't owe me a damn thing. But I'd appreciate it if you could do this one thing for me."

Stephanie took the letter from Jeremy. "Thank you so much," she whispered.

"Just wait until my signal. Then get the kid the hell out of here."

Jeremy turned and walked out of the office. He didn't lock the door behind him and walked down the hallway. Stephanie looked down at Tyler sleeping. She had no choice but to trust Jeremy. She was worried about getting set up. The fact that he entrusted her to give his mom a letter from him suggested to Stephanie that she could trust him. All she had to do know was wait on Jeremy's signal.

She looked down at Tyler as he slept on her lap. "It'll be okay," she whispered to him.

Client Privilege

Jack and Dale were back to square one. They were at the courtyard, stumped. The same person that had been following them over the city was their killer.

"I'm getting fed up with this fucking shit," Dale said.

"Welcome to homicide, kid. What do you think we should do now?" Jack asked.

He wanted to see if Dale was still up to the task of being on this case. He was concerned about his health and his judgment. Him pulling his gun on O'Malley frightened him.

Dale was holding his side and breathing heavy again. Jack was going to have to tell Cappy to take Dale off the case.

"Dulaney is our best bet. He knows more than he's telling us. *Fuck* attorney-client privilege."

Jack was impressed with Dale's response. He nodded his head yes. "Sometimes in life, you have to play dirty to get a clean victory," Jack said to Dale. "So what do you want to do?"

Dale looked at Jack with determination. "Let's play," Dale said.

Jack smiled. Dale returned with a smirk of his own.

They walked back to their car. A patrolman was on the scene. He ran over to Jack and Dale in front of the building. They showed the officer their badges.

"Detectives Prescott and Harding, homicide. Secure the scene and call the medical examiner and CSI team," Jack said to the officer.

He didn't even wait for the officer to say anything. They didn't even bother waiting for the corner or CSI people to show up. Their next move was Dulaney. Jack knew he was involved. They just had to figure out a way to break him.

Dale got in the car. Jack was on his phone outside the car. He finally got in. "Who was that?" Dale asked.

Jack looked over at him with a smile and smirked. "I think I found our way in."

It was nearly midnight when they got to Dulaney's brownstone. His car was parked outside his place. Jack parked their car across the street. It was getting dark outside as the streetlights came on.

Dale was moving around in the passenger seat, holding his side again. Jack looked over to see if he was okay. He reached in and took out Dale's pill bottle. He handed Dale a pill. Dale quickly grabbed the pill and took it without any hesitation.

"How are you feeling?" Jack asked.

"Like shit," Dale replied.

"Well, after we find the girl and kid and figure out who is trying to kill us, you're going to take some time off."

"Oh, don't forget about Derek Conway," Dale added.

"He is probably at the bottom of the Hudson for all we know. Getting Stephanie and the kid back is our number one priority."

"So what are we sitting here waiting for?" Dale asked.

"Just a routine stakeout. You never know what will happen," Jack replied as he stared at Dulaney's brownstone.

Dale knew Jack was up to something. Whatever it was, it was nothing good. All Dale could do at this point is wait and follow Jack's lead. Jack kept looking at his watch and looking at Dulaney's brownstone.

It was after midnight. Dulaney was pacing back and forth in his house on his cell phone. "You promised me that this would be a clean job. Quick and easy payday. Now all the sudden, I have the NYPD on my ass, asking me about my clients that you hired."

Dulaney was more frantic than ever. "Yeah, well, you tell the big boss that I'm done. I don't want any more part of this. You already whacked Warrick. I won't be next." He hung up his phone and went to the kitchen.

Dulaney went and got a bottle of whiskey from his lower cabinet. He poured a glass nearly full. He was stressed about being involved with the kidnapping and murders. He was now more concerned that the police had him under their radar.

Dulaney knew it was a matter of time before he was caught. He walked back into the living room with his glass. He sat in his leather chair to watch TV. He was hoping that would calm his nerves.

It was nearly 1:00 AM. Dulaney had nearly finished his third glass of whiskey. His eyes were getting heavy. The glare from the TV didn't faze him. He finally closed his eyes.

Dulaney was out for about two hours. He was sleeping like a baby. All of a sudden, a masked man put his hand over his mouth. Dulaney gasped for air. He struggled to get away but couldn't.

The masked man picked up Dulaney and threw him across the living room. He crawled to the kitchen to get away from his attacker. Dulaney feared the worst; he was going to be killed like Warrick. Dulaney knew too much.

The masked man picked up the lamp from Dulaney's stand. He slowly walked behind Dulaney as he was crawling for his life. He raised up the lamp to hit Dulaney. "Please, I won't say anything," Dulaney pleaded. "I'll do whatever you want."

Jack and Dale busted through the front door. The masked man ran through the kitchen. Jack ran after the attacker. Dale ran over to check on Dulaney. "Are you all right?" Dale asked.

"I'm fine," Dulaney replied.

Dulaney had an opened wound on the side of his temple. Dale helped get Dulaney up and walked him over to the couch. "Do you need medical attention?" Dale asked.

"Oh gee, what the fuck to you think?" Dulaney asked. "I'm fucking bleeding."

Jack walked back into the living room. He slowly walked over to the couch and sat next to Dulaney. He had a smirk on his face. Dulaney was wondering what Jack was smiling about.

"We know you're involved with the Lambert kidnapping. We know you're involved with Keith Warrick's murder. So now, Mr. Lawyer, this is the time to make a deal."

Jack was confident. Dulaney knew he was in trouble. "I don't know what the fuck you're talking about. Now could one of you people call an ambulance and put out an APB on that fucker who tried to kill me?" Dulaney demanded.

"You don't know what I'm talking about?" Jack asked. "Funny, the man who came in here and tried to kill you resembles one of the men who tried to kill two NYPD detectives and kidnap two people. I find that to be a huge coincidence. It was a long road. A mystery man murdered. Two people kidnapped for an unknown reason. A murdered parole officer. And his list of parolees that we think are involved led us right to you."

Dulaney had a blank look on his face. Dale was just sitting there, watching Jack play dirty.

"It'll be best if you just tell us what you know. We know you're involved somehow," Dale said. "That man almost killed you. Next time, you will not be so lucky. I think he came here to shut up like they did with Keith Warrick."

"Just stop!" Dulaney shouted. "I get it. I don't know a lot."

Jack leaned closer to Dulaney. "Tell us what you do know."

"I can't. You don't know who you're dealing with," Dulaney said.

"I have an idea," Jack replied. "Tell us what you know. You really don't want me to say it again."

"Before I say anything, I want protection," Dulaney demanded. "You put me into protective custody, and I'll cooperate."

Jack and Dale looked up at each other. Jack was concerned about who was involved. Dulaney was an experienced defense attorney. He's been threatened many times by clients. It was part of the game. The fact that he wants protection before he says anything told Jack that he was legit scared.

"I'll talk to my captain," Jack said.

"That's not good enough. I'm a dead man. I know little about what's going on. Imagine if I knew more." Dulaney was scared out of his mind.

"We'll protect you," Jack said.

"Spill it," Dale said.

"Warrick approached me about three months ago. He gave me a list of his parolees and asked me to tell him the names of my clients. I told him no. He gave me an envelope."

"What was in it?" Dale asked.

"Somehow, Warrick found out that I was double billing my clients."

"I always knew defense attorneys were frauds. I didn't know it was for real," Jack added. "What else?"

"I asked him how he knew about that. He said the boss has his ways. I told him only three of my clients were on his list."

"What did he want you to do?" Dale asked.

"He called them up and told them about a job. I asked what the job was. He told me to rent a white van and he would take care of the rest. After I saw the shooting at the Sheridan and the kidnapping of the girl and kid, I put it together."

"Why did Warrick want them kidnapped?" Jack asked.

"I don't know," Dulaney replied.

"Who was this boss?" Dale asked.

"I don't know."

"Who is Derek Conway?" Jack asked.

"I don't know."

"Well, whatever you do know was enough to get you killed. That's why they eliminated Warrick. He was the middleman. This boss is tying up loose ends. Did Warrick say what the backup plan was if anything went south?" Jack asked.

"Warrick said his partner promised them all a clean-paying job. He gave me a number to call if anything were to happen. I just got off the phone with him before you showed up."

"Who is he?" Dale asked.

"He didn't say. His voice was disguised too. I'm supposed to meet him tomorrow morning at Grand Central to give me my money."

"Okay then, tomorrow it is," Jack said.

Dulaney was confused. "How the hell are you going to catch him when you don't know what he looks like?" he asked.

"He knows what you look like," Dale added.

"What the fuck are you talking about?"

"We're going fishing. And you're going to be the bait," Jack said. "He finds you and we nail him. Hopefully can lead us to Stephanie and Tyler."

Jack got up from the couch and walked toward the kitchen. "Go get some clothes and go out to the car. I'll be right back."

Dale helped Dulaney upstairs to get a change of clothes. Jack walked through the kitchen and out the back door. The masked attacker was waiting for Jack by the kitchen door.

Jack walked out of the door onto the back patio. "It worked like a charm. You can keep that mask on. You look better with it."

"Fuck you," the masked man said. He took off the mask. It was Eight-Ball. "You owe me big fucking time," he said to Jack.

"Yeah, I get that a lot. Thanks a lot. Stay low," Jack said.

"Stay low? What the fuck you talking about, Jackie? I always hang low."

"Get the fuck out of here," Jack said. He walked back into Dulaney's brownstone. He met Dulaney and Dale coming down the stairs. Dulaney had a suitcase with him.

"When we get to the station, we'll get that head looked at," Dale said.

"Then get some rest. Tomorrow we end this."

The Meet

It was 7:00 AM. Dulaney had on an orange polo shirt and tan khaki pants. He has never been used in a sting operation before. Cappy wasn't too thrilled with the whole thing. A part of him wanted to jump across his desk and beat Dulaney to a pulp. He could sense Cappy staring him down as he sat at the table in his office.

Jack came in with Dale. "Lift up your shirt," Jack said. They were taping a wire to Dulaney's chest. Dulaney was getting more nervous.

"What if he doesn't show up?" Dulaney asked.

"If he does, you're both going to jail. If he doesn't, you're going to jail," Cappy said. He never took his eyes off Dulaney. He just stared a hole right through him.

Sims came walking into Cappy's office. "Everything is good to go," she said.

"How's Kennedy?" Dale asked.

"He's good. I informed him on everything. He's not too happy to be stuck in a hospital bed."

Cappy's phone rang. "Yeah?" he answered. "Thanks. The tech guys said you're coming in loud and clear," he said to Dulaney. "Which means if you tip this guy off or say even one punctuation wrong, we'll be all over you like ugly on your mama. Are we clear?"

"Yeah, crystal clear."

"Okay, Jack will be the primary. Don't be more than twenty feet from him. Dale, you're the backup. Sims, cover the main entrance. I'll have units posted on the platform and small exits. We can't cover every exit strategy without tipping this guy off. Keep a lookout for Polk, Jensen, and Goldstein."

"They won't be there," Jack said to Cappy.

"Whoever this boss is, he's too smart. He knows we're already looking for those three. That's why he's meeting Dulaney in a massive public place. We don't know who he is, but he knows who we are. It's the perfect conceal. I doubt he even shows up."

"Why don't you think he'll show up?" Sims asked.

"The perfect conceal, like I said. Besides, if he doesn't show, I have a feeling is because we will recognize him."

"You think we have another dirty cop?" Dale asked.

"Why else would Internal Affairs be breathing down our necks?" Jack asked.

"Okay, that's enough," Cappy said. He sat at his desk. The last thing he wanted to hear was more dirty cop talk. "Just get this piece of shit out of here and end this fucking mess."

"I didn't mean for this to happen," Dulaney said.

"Yeah, well, one of my detectives is in the hospital. I have a dead parole officer, an unknown dead guy we're still trying to find. We have two kidnapped people that we're trying to figure out why. A possible dirty cop in my unit. And so far, you're the only one that's been caught. You better pray that man shows up and that woman and kid are safe. I'd hate to see how a lawyer would be in prison."

Dulaney stood up and walked to the door. He turned and looked at Cappy. "For what it's worth, I am sorry for all this."

Cappy just sat there. Dale escorted Dulaney through the squad room. Jack stayed behind to talk to Cappy. Sims followed Dale and Dulaney and closed the door behind her.

"Do you really think there's a dirty cop in our unit?" Cappy asked.

"Yes," Jack answered. "We need to find the girl and kid first, then we can worry about this fucking rat. You call the FBI or Marshal's?"

"Fuck them! This is our case. Let's just get this guy and go from there."

Jack felt like Cappy wasn't in the right state of mind. He is usually a team player. He felt distant from him. This case had everybody in an uproar. Everybody never recovered from the Badger.

They pulled up to the station. Jack leaned back to Dulaney. He put his hand on Dulaney's chest to cover the microphone. "Just so you realize, if you fuck this up in any way, I will put a bullet in your right ass cheek," Jack said.

"I don't know if I can go through with this," Dulaney said.

Dale was concerned that Dulaney could pull this off. He was shaking and very anxious. Jack was getting annoyed with the whole thing.

"You need to calm the fuck down," Jack demanded.

Dulaney took a couple deep breaths. He got out of the car and slowly walked into the station. There were crowds of people rushing in and out of the station. Dulaney quickly disappeared into the crowd.

Jack and Dale got out of the car and slowly walked into the station. It was congested. Jack and Dale were trying to push their way through to the station.

Dulaney made his way to the lower level. Sims was by a newsstand, waiting for him. Dulaney made eye contact with Sims. He knew he was being watched.

Cappy had a radio on his desk. He was listening to every word that was said. There was a tech crew down the street from the station listening to Dulaney. Cappy wanted this man caught more than anything.

Dulaney was standing by the ticket counter. Jack and Dale stood against the wall. Jack was staring a hole through Dulaney. Dale was looking at all the people walking by Dulaney.

"You see anybody familiar?" Jack asked.

Dale was scouring with eyes to anybody walking by Dulaney. Dulaney was looking around as well. So far, nobody caught their eyes. Jack didn't trust Dulaney at all. He was more worried that this was going to be an escape plan for him than waiting for the big boss to show up.

Cappy was sitting on the edge of his chair in his office. All he could hear was the people in the background.

"I don't see anybody," Dulaney said.

"Shut the fuck up, idiot. If the moneyman sees you moving your lips, he's going to know something's up," Jack said.

Sims saw some young guy walking around the corner. He had on a navy blue sweatshirt and black sweatpants and a black backpack. He stood out like a sore thumb. "I may have something," Sims said. "White male, five foot ten, blue sweatshirt and black sweatpants, black backpack."

Jack and Dale looked down the terminal to find the guy. They could see him from afar, walking down the terminal toward them. Dulaney looked to see him coming.

"This may be the deliveryman. Don't blow it," Jack said to Dulaney.

Dulaney took in a deep breath. He hadn't been this nervous since he took the bar exam. Even then, he wasn't this nervous.

The guy with the backpack stopped in front of Dulaney. He looked around to see if they were being watched. He didn't notice Jack, Dale, or even Sims from afar. Dulaney just stood there. He didn't know what to say or do.

"This fucker is smart," Jack said. "Sending a currier to the meet. He really doesn't want to be seen."

"I still don't get why he's getting paid," Dale added.

"What do you mean?" Jack asked.

"Look at him. That poor bastard is terrified. He literally thought we were going to kill him last night. Now all of a sudden they're going to pay this guy? For what?"

"Jesus Christ," Jack said. "How much you want to bet that there's no money in that backpack?"

"It's a bomb," Dale said.

"What?" Jack asked.

"It's a bomb. I've been nearly blown up enough times to know when there's a bomb lurking."

"Pop, it's a trap," he said to Cappy as he was trying to get to Dulaney. "Dulaney, get away from him."

Dulaney didn't hear Jack. The guy sat the backpack down in front of Dulaney and walked away. Dulaney reached down to pick up the backpack.

Jack couldn't get Dulaney's attention. He pulled out his gun to fire a warning shot. Dulaney reached down to grab the backpack. The backpack exploded, killing Dulaney instantly.

The crowd in the station panicked with fear. They were running in every direction. Jack was fighting his way through the crowd to get to Dulaney.

"Sims, try to get out to the street and try to find the delivery boy," Jack shouted.

Jack finally made it over to Dulaney. It was too late. The shock wave from the explosion crushed his chest. He had burns all over him. Dale fought his way over to them. Jack sat down next to Dulaney's body. He felt so defeated.

Their only lead was dead. The big boss was still out there. Stephanie and Tyler were no closer to being found.

Deadline

Cappy raced to Grand Central. It was so crowded he had to fight his through to the entrance. He was stopped by guards at the main door. Cappy showed them his badge and was escorted to the crime scene.

The bomb squad and the CSI team were there. Cappy saw Jack standing over the remains of Dulaney's body. Dale and Sims were getting checked by the EMTs. He walked over to Jack.

"What the hell happened?" Cappy asked.

"We were set up," Jack said as he stared at Dulaney's body.

"What the hell do you mean set up?"

"Somebody told somebody about our plan and took care of it. This guy is too smart to come into a crowded place. Dulaney was never going to get paid. He sent a deliveryman in to kill me him and even a few others just for the hell of it."

Cappy was so distraught. He didn't know what to do anymore with the fact that not only was he determined to find Stephanie and Tyler but also now the possibility of having a rat in his unit.

"What's the plan, Pop?" Jack asked.

"I don't know."

Jack looked behind Cappy and saw Lieutenant Graham walking toward them. "Oh shit!"

Cappy turned around and saw Graham coming toward them. He knew what Graham was going to tell them.

"Well, Detective Prescott, what a fucking surprise," Graham said as he clapped his hands. "With all the gunfights and explosions lately, we're going to have to start calling you Bruce Willis."

"Skip the sarcasm, and tell us why you're here," Cappy demanded.

"Well, let's see. First off, there was the Sheridan. Then there was the group home and then the kidnapping that left one officer in the hospital and now a dead attorney. Oh, there was a murder late yesterday in Midtown. I'm assuming that was you also. You have made no arrests and apparently no leads. Apparently, the only thing good solid lead you had is lying in pieces all over the *goddamn* floor!"

Dale and Sims walked over to Graham. They couldn't help but hear his voice carry, along with the ringing in their ears, from the explosion.

"So this is how it goes. As of midnight tonight, you and your entire squad are off the case. Agent Temple will lead the investigation. Also, starting tomorrow morning, each one of you, including you, Captain, will undergo a psychological evaluation pending a full Internal Affairs investigation."

"You can't do that," Cappy said.

"Oh, yes, I can. And I already have. I pulled every one of your files personally. You probably should've stayed retired, old timer."

Cappy made a fist with his hand. He wanted so hard to hit Graham in the face. Jack grabbed Cappy's arm to restrain him.

"So if by some miracle that you not only find the girl and kid but also find the people responsible within the next fourteen hours, I would prepare for a nice long vacation. Have a good day, lady and gentlemen."

Graham walked away with a smirk on his face. Cappy was so mad that he was shaking. Jack patted his back to calm him down.

"What the hell was that all about?" Sims asked.

"We're *fucked*, that what that means," Jack said.

"What's our next move?" Dale asked.

Cappy just stood there with his hands on his hips. He looked down at Dulaney's body as the coroner's assistants were gathering his remains. He was on the verge of a mental break.

"I'll have the crime scene unit gather as much as they can. The bomb squad is on the way. I'll have them see if there is anything on the explosives used. Sims and Dale, go to the security office. Go through every piece of footage and try to find the delivery guy."

Sims and Dale walked down the terminal to find the security office. Cappy walked in the opposite direction. Jack walked with him.

"How bad is it?" Jack asked.

"Bad enough that I almost hit the bottle again."

"Jesus Christ, Pop. You can't do that."

"You think I don't know that?" Cappy asked. He sighed as he walked down the platform.

"So what's the worst that can happen?" Jack asked.

"The girl dies. The kid dies. I lose my command. You get busted to meter maid at best. Dale gets transferred. Internal Affairs finds some dirt on one of us and destroys our credibility. Ya know, shit like that."

Jack smirked at Cappy. Cappy smiled back as he looked at his watch.

"I wouldn't trust anybody more than I would with you. You're like my own son. Do you think we can solve this before midnight tonight?" Cappy asked.

Jack looked Cappy in his eyes. Cappy knew that look. It was Jack's motivation and determination that drove him to be an outstanding cop.

"I know we can," Jack replied.

Cappy sighed in relief. He smiled at Jack. Deep down, he knew Jack and his team could find Stephanie and Tyler and find out who took them and why.

Jack turned and walked toward the main entrance of the terminal. He turned and looked at Cappy. "Whatever it takes?" he asked him.

"Whatever it takes," Cappy replied.

Jack went outside and saw Andrea Bailey behind the caution tape. Jack knew she would be there. She was a vulture when it came to reporting news. Anytime something happens in the city, she is there. Jack despised reporters but admired her passion.

He saw her among the other news reporters. Jack walked over to her. Typical Andrea, stuck a microphone in front is his face. "Detective! Can you tell us anything about what on here? Was there any civilian casualties?"

Jack grabbed her arm and dragged her away from the crowd. They walked over to a line of buses that were parked along the curb.

"Okay, what do you have for me?" Jack asked.

"C'mon, Detective, that's not a pleasant way to ask for a favor," she replied.

"I'm not in the mood for games nor do I have time. We've got until midnight to find the girl and kid. We are on a deadline. Do you understand me? Now please tell me what you have for me."

"Let's take a walk to my office."

Jack followed Andrea to her van. They snuck past the crowd of reporters and civilians. Her cameraman followed them. Jack looked around to see if anybody was watching. They got into her van.

Andrea reached into the front seat and grabbed a folder and handed it to Jack. "Ta-da!" she said with a smile on her face.

"What do you have?" Jack asked as he opened the folder.

"So I couldn't find one solid lead with your white van. There were too many to find, and since you were crunched for time, I went on to my next best bet. I contacted a friend of mine who works in real estate. I got all the properties within a five-hundred-mile radius that were rented out or sold within the last six months. I figured if I was a kidnapper and wanted to not be seen, I wouldn't be here in the city where law enforcement was swarming."

Jack started looking through all the properties and throwing them away one by one.

"What are you doing?" Andrea asked.

"The asswipes who took the girl and kid aren't in the city. I'm only interested in the properties outside of the city."

Jack found the nine properties north of the city. He knew they didn't have time to investigate them all. He had to narrow it down. "Thanks for the help," Jack said as he got out of the van.

"Hey, wait a minute. You promised me an exclusive."

"If your real estate friend came through, then you will."

Jack walked back into the terminal. He went to the security office to see if Sims and Dale had any luck with getting the delivery-man on tape. He walked by the gurney that had Dulaney on it.

All he could think of is guilt for much of what has happened. Every lead turned to either a dead end or another dead body. He always wondered if he was losing is edge that made him a good cop.

Jack went into the security office. Sims and Dale were sitting in front of a wall of camera monitors. Two security officers were sitting on each side of them. They were playing back the footage from the time the bomb exploded.

"You find anything?" Jack asked.

"Nothing yet. We have different camera angles all over the terminal. Nothing solid yet," Sims said.

Jack leaned down to look at the monitors as well. He was looking at the area where Dulaney was standing. He watched the explosion on the monitors. He saw the delivery guy on one of the monitors.

"Stop!" he yelled. "Monitor eleven."

He saw the deliveryman running out of the terminal. The security officer rewound the tape and paused it on his face. "Print that out and run that through every database we have," Jack said to Sims.

Sims took the photo from the printer and rushed back to the station to run it through the database for a match.

Dale followed Jack out of the security office. Dale grabbed his side again.

"How are you holding up?" Jack asked.

Dale had a disgusted look on his face. "I'll be fine."

Jack reached into his pocket and got out Dale's pill bottle. Dale looked at Jack's hand, waiting for his dose. Jack handed the entire bottle to him. Dale was in an amazement.

"Is this your way of saying I trust you?" Dale asked.

"No, this is my way of saying I need you," Jack replied. "We only have thirteen hours to solve this case. I don't need a pained drug-addicted angry rookie. I need a partner. Can I count on you?"

Dale put the pills in his pocket. "What's up with the folder?" Dale asked.

"A gift from a friend. A list of all the properties rented or sold within the last six months. It's not much, but if I was these guys, I'd be staying outside the city."

"So what's the move?"

"Until Sims hopefully gets some answers, we're going to go into the real estate business."

Jack and Dale left the train station. They got into the car. Dale took the folder and looked inside. "We're going to search all these?" Dale asked.

"No, just the ones outside the city. Start from about one hundred miles north," Jack said.

Dale looked at the listings and the map that was enclosed. "Looks like…Unionport, New York. About two hours' drive north of here. An old warehouse in the center of town."

"Let's do it," Jack said as he drove away from the train station.

"So after we get there, we're down to about ten hours. What happens if your hunch is wrong?" Dale asked.

"Then we're *fucked*."

Real Estate

It was just before noon when Jack and Dale reached the town of Unionport. It looked like a quiet town. Dale was amazed on how it was the complete opposite from the city. Peaceful and stress free.

"This town looks too good to be true," Dale said.

"That's probably because it is," Jack replied. "There's the warehouse."

Jack and Dale pulled up to the warehouse. There were no signs of anybody inside. Jack was hoping that there were people inside.

"I don't think I can handle another goddamn warehouse," Jack said as he got out of the car. He looked up and down the street and didn't see anything out of the ordinary.

Dale reached into his pocket and took out his pill bottle. Jack turned and gave Dale a look of disdain.

"Relax, I'm only taking one." Dale showed Jack one pill and took it in front of him. He saw Dale put the bottle back into his pocket.

"What do you think the odds are of finding Stephanie and Tyler in there?" Dale asked.

Jack walked up to the front door of the warehouse. "Slim to none. If I were the kidnappers, I would want privacy and discretion, not be in the middle of town."

Jack tried to look in the side window of the warehouse. It was pitch-dark. Dale went and got two flashlights out of the trunk of the car. He gave one to Jack.

"You're really going to break into the building?" Dale asked. "We don't even have a warrant."

"Call a cop," Jack replied.

"I'm going to check around back," Dale said.

Jack wasn't being discreet at all. They had less than twelve hours to find Stephanie and Tyler before the feds take over. As determined as he was to finding them, he was trying harder to not let Cappy down.

Jack waited for a few minutes to see if Dale had any luck. The front door opened. "I take it the back door was open," Jack said.

"No, I kicked the door in," Dale replied.

"You law-breaking son of a bitch."

"Yeah, well, I'm a fast learner."

Dale opened the door for Jack. He turned his flashlight on. The warehouse was empty. "This brings back memories," Jack said. "The only thing that'll put the icing on this shit cake is to be attacked from behind again."

Jack heard a sound behind him. It was the sound of the hammer being pulled on a gun. They slowly raised their hands up. "Speak of the devil," Dale said.

"You're under arrest for trespassing on private property. Drop your lights and let me see those armpits."

Jack quickly lowered his hands down. "Thank fucking Christ!" he said.

He turned around and saw an older man in a sheriff uniform. "You the sheriff?" Jack asked.

"I SAID RAISE YOUR HANDS!" He pointed his revolver at Jack. With everything that he has been through in the last month, this was a sigh of relief for him.

"Relax, Sheriff. We're on the job," Jack explained.

Dale still had his hands in the air. "NYPD," Dale said.

The sheriff wasn't trusting of them. "Let me see some credentials." He pointed his revolver over at Dale. "You, pretty boy. You first."

Jack smirked at the sheriff for that remark. Dale rolled his eyes. He slowly reached into this pocket and pulled out his badge.

The sheriff slowly lowered his gun. Jack reached under his hoodie and pulled out his shield. "You're in charge around here?" Jack asked.

"Sheriff Hagerty. I heard pretty boy over say you're NYPD?"

"Please quit calling me that," Dale pleaded.

"Shut up, pretty boy," Jack said. "Yeah. You hear about the Amber Alert in Manhattan?"

"Yeah, my office got the notice yesterday. What about it?" Hagerty asked.

"Do you think you could put your gun away?" Dale asked.

"Oh yeah, sorry."

Hagerty lowered his gun and put it back in its holster. Dale finally lowered his hands and slowly walked over to Jack.

"So again, why is the NYPD breaking into a building in my town?" Hagerty asked.

"We have reason to believe that the kidnappers may be around here somewhere."

"Wait a damn minute. I know every person in this town. I know what goes on here day and night. We are a peaceful community. There's no way they are here."

Hagerty was livid and stormed outside. Jack and Dale just stood there in the dark warehouse.

"So does this mean we're off the hook?" Dale asked.

Jack rolled his eyes and walked out to find Hagerty. He was standing in front of his patrol car with his arms crossed. Jack and Dale walked over to him. Jack leaned up against Hagerty's car.

"I'm sorry for the intrusion. I'd be pissy too if I found two out-of-town cops who obviously don't abide by the dress code breaking into one of my buildings. But we need your help. We have a ticking clock. Now let's quit comparing dick sizes and work together, huh?"

"What do you need to know?" Hagerty asked.

Jack took out the property listings that Andrea gave him. He put them on the hood of Hagerty's cruiser.

"You know more about these areas than we do," Jack said. "Help us out. Do you know any of these properties?"

Hagerty studied the listings. Jack stood next to Hagerty. He hovered over his shoulder, hoping he would find something to help them out. Hagerty pointed to a listing.

"I'm not too sure about this one. It's an old abandoned paper factory right outside of Bradley township. It's about fifty miles north of here. If I were a kidnapper, that would be as good as a secluded place as any to hide somebody. The rest of the properties are up in the Catskills and near the border."

Jack nodded his head. It was the only good solid lead they had. He had no choice to but to follow through with Hagerty's suggestion. This was possibly their last shot on finding Stephanie and Tyler.

"You know the police in Bradley that could help us?" Jack asked.

"They're not that good. What can I do to help?" Hagerty asked.

"How many men do you have?" Dale asked Hagerty.

"I have seven deputies. Put if I make a few calls, I can have the county tactical team geared up and ready to deploy within the hour."

Jack and Dale looked at each other. They knew it wasn't much to go on. "Make the call," Jack said.

Hagerty had a smile on his face. "There's a rest stop just outside of Bradley township. Meet me there in an hour."

Hagerty got into his car and drove toward town. Jack and Dale got into their car and drove north.

"You think they're hiding up there?" Dale asked.

"It's our last shot. So yes, I'm hoping that they're up there."

Fault

Stephanie paced back and forth in the office. She was anxious to see how Jeremy was going to help them. Tyler was curled up on the couch, watching Stephanie. It's been awhile since Jeremy was gone.

"I'm scared," Tyler uttered.

It got her attention. She walked over to the couch and sat next to him. "I'm scared too, sweetheart," Stephanie replied. "I won't let anything happen to you, I promise."

"Is that man going to help us?" Tyler asked.

Stephanie was trying to not cry again. She grabbed him and held him close to her. "I hope so, honey. I hope so."

Jeremy was down by the van. He was guarding the complex to make sure there were no intruders. He was trying to figure out a way to get Stephanie and Tyler out of there.

The only way he could see it was he had to steal the van to make their escape. He didn't have the keys. And there wasn't a subtle way to sneak them past the other two masked men. He had to take the keys and go from there.

Jeremy walked back up to the top floor. He walked into the first room at the top of the stairs. There were two men sitting at a table, watching TV. It was Polk and Jensen.

"He got Dulaney," Polk said.

"Who did?" Jeremy asked.

"Ronnie," Jensen said. "He wasn't kidding about taking extreme precautions."

"So am I ever going to meet him?" Jeremy asked.

They just ignored him. "When am I going to get my money?"

"Just go back to your post," Jensen said.

Jeremy wasn't going to get the keys that easy. He knew Polk and Jensen weren't going to let their guard down. He went back out the door and walked down the steps to the van.

"We're going to have to fix that problem," Jensen told Polk.

Jeremy went back to the van. He was stumped. He didn't know how to hot-wire a car, so that theory was out the window. It was two miles to the main road, so he couldn't signal somebody without being missed.

The only way he could see around it was that he was going to have to make a distraction to lure Polk and Jensen away. It was getting late into the day. Jeremy had to act fast to make this work.

He had an idea. Set the place on fire. The smoke would alert somebody to come and investigate. It would also lure Polk and Jensen away from their post so he could sneak Stephanie and Tyler out.

Jeremy went to the other side of the factory and got some old dry paper from the assembly lines. He was just acting on impulse. He put some paper in the corner and lit a fire. Jeremy quickly went back to the van.

He waited for the smell of smoke to make his move. Minutes went by and very faintly could smell something burning. He slowly walked back into the plant to see how much the fire had spread.

The fire was spreading through the lower floor of the factory. The smoke was getting thicker. Jeremy started coughing. This was his move. He raced up to the top floor to let Polk and Jensen know there was a fire.

He opened the door and saw Polk and Jensen standing there with another masked man. "There's a fire downstairs," Jeremy said.

They all just stood there staring at him. Jeremy didn't know what was going on.

"Who is this?" Jeremy asked.

The masked man took out a gun with a silencer on it and shot Jeremy in the head. Polk and Jensen were stunned. They didn't think he would do it right there. "That wasn't part of the plan," Polk yelled.

He walked over Jeremy's body to the hallway. "Bring him," he said as he walked toward the office where Stephanie and Tyler were at.

Polk and Jensen dragged Jeremy's body down the hallway to the office. The masked man opened the door and let Polk and Jensen drag Jeremy's body into the office.

Stephanie screamed. She shielded Tyler's eyes from seeing it. The masked man pointed his gun at them. She looked at him with so much anger and fear she wanted to lunge at him.

He aimed his gun at Jeremy and shot him again in the chest. Tyler screamed. Stephanie could feel Tyler shaking against her. The masked man walked over to her and leaned down toward her.

"This is your fault. His blood is on your hands," he whispered. He turned and walked out with Polk and Jensen, leaving Jeremy's body in the office with Stephanie and Tyler.

She held him as she watched the blood pour out of Jeremy. She was defeated. Their only hope of getting out of there was now gone.

The masked man walked back into the office at the top of the steps. "Now what?" Polk asked.

He turned and looked at them. "Put out the fire. It's going to attract people. Then move them to the alternate location." He then walked out of the room and left the factory. Polk and Jensen were confused on what just happened.

"What the hell is going on?" Polk asked.

"He lost his shit, that's what," Jensen replied.

Lost and Found

Jack and Dale were parked at the rest stop just outside of Bradley township. They were waiting on Hagerty to arrive. They were concerned about involving a small-town sheriff with a case like this.

Jack wasn't too sure how this was going to go down. He had doubts that they were never going to find them. The only thing Jack had right now was his instincts. His instincts were telling him that they will find Stephanie and Tyler alive and find out who was behind not only their kidnapping but multiple murders as well.

"You think we'll find them?" Dale asked.

Jack just paced back and forth beside the car. Jack looked at his watch. "It's time for your pill."

Dale crossed his arms and leaned up against the car. "We'll find them," Dale said.

He walked over to Jack and patted him on his back. "We will find them. And we will catch these fuckers who did this."

Jack saw a line of cars driving toward the rest stop. It was Hagerty. Jack walked over to meet them. They pulled into the parking lot of the rest stop. Hagerty had three deputies and the county tactical team with them.

"Sorry I was late. I had to take a shit," Hagerty said.

He pulled out some papers from his car. He laid them out on the hood of his car. "Called in a favor. I always wanted to use that line," Hagerty said with amusement. "I got the old architectural plans from the paper factory."

Jack and Dale looked over the plans. Hagerty leaned over them to study with them. "To tell you the truth, I've never done anything like this before," Hagerty told them.

"You have a SWAT team with you. They can handle it," Dale said.

Hagerty introduced the leader of the tactical team. "This is Sergeant Bowman. He's in charge of the tactical team."

"Have you done any breach situations before?" Jack asked.

"To be honest, no," Bowman replied.

Jack just rubbed his temples and tried not to lose what little composure he had left. "Okay, with that being said," Jack said as he walked back to Hagerty's car.

"From what I can see, there are two entry points into this factory. One, the main entrance to the factory. One team will cover that and sweep that floor. Team two will come with me to the back of the factory. There's an office building that connects to the factory. We will take the back door and sweep the office floor by floor."

"I'll lead the other team," Dale suggested.

"You, Bowman, and his team will take the main entrance. I'll take Hagerty and his deputies and take the offices," Jack said to Dale.

"There's a back road that's along the back side of the factory. That's probably our best bet to being stealthy," Hagerty said.

"I agree with that," Jack said. "We'll take that road and come in from the back. Dale, you take your team and come in the main entrance."

"How many assailants are we dealing with here?" Bowman asked.

"At least three that we know of," Dale said. "There could be more. But we're just not sure."

"Make sure everybody has body armor and loaded weapons. They've shot at us and tried to blow us up. Our number one priority is to find the girl and kid. Let's get ready to move out," Jack said.

One of Bowman's men came running up to him. "Sir, We just got a call from the Bradley Township Fire Department. People reports smoke coming from the old paper factory."

"LET'S MOVE OUT!" Bowman yelled.

Everybody raced to their cars. "Tell the fire department to come in silent until we know for sure if they're in there or not," Jack said to Bowman.

Dale went with Bowman and his team. Jack got into his car and raced toward the factory. Hagerty and his deputies were right behind him.

Jack's cell phone rang. "Prescott," he answered.

"It's Sims. I got a positive ID on the delivery boy from the station. His name was Kyle Johansen. He did some time in Attica for grand theft auto. Got released six months ago. He's probably the one who got ahold of the white van. I checked his taxes. Seems he had a job as, get this, a pizza delivery boy. Some pizza place in Bradley township called Papa Tony's Specialty Pizza."

"DAMN!" Jack yelled.

"What is it?" Sims asked.

"That's where we are. We think that Stephanie and Tyler are up here. Let Cappy know. It's an old paper factory on the outskirts of Bradley township."

Jack hung up the phone and raced to get to the factory. That was no coincidence that Johansen worked up here. His instincts were right. They used Johansen to scout the area, looking for places to hide out. Then killed him when he wasn't needed. The same with Warrick and Dulaney.

Jack could see the smoke coming from over the hills. They were getting close. They went on the back road that Hagerty suggested. They stopped and parked their cars on the road. They could see the factory through the trees.

Hagerty and his deputies got out and met over at Jack's car. "The factory is right there," Hagerty said.

"Okay, we go in nice and quiet. There's a lot of windows in that office building. I'll take the top floor. You guys take the other four. Watch yourselves." Jack pulled out his gun and ran through the trees to the back of the factory.

Haggerty and his men followed right behind. They all had their body armor and guns drawn. The fire was starting to grow throughout the building. Jack opened the back door of the office building and went inside. Hagerty and his men followed.

Dale and his team pulled into the main entrance of the factory. Dale saw a white van parked by the main door. "They're here," Dale said. "Get your men. We're going in," he said to Bowman.

They got out of the tactical team van and drew their guns. Dale ducked down and quietly ran over toward the white van. He felt the engine to see if had been recently on. The hood was cold.

Dale went inside the factory. There was smoke throughout the building. Dale had trouble seeing in front of him. Bowman walked in behind Dale. His men had flashlights on their assault rifles to see better. Dale started coughing from the smoke.

Polk heard Dale coughing. He turned and started shooting through the smoke. "GET DOWN!" Dale yelled. The smoke was thick and nobody couldn't see. Dale and Bowman returned fire. Polk shot back.

Jack heard the shots from the other side of the building. "I'll check the floors. You go and help them," Jack said. Hagerty and his team raced through the burning building to assist Dale's team.

Jack searched the first floor of the office building and didn't find anything. He knew Stephanie and Tyler were there. He just wished there were still alive.

Hagerty and his deputies fought their way through the smoke to Dale. They could hear gun fire from afar. Dale and Bowman were firing their weapons through the smoke. "POLICE! DROP YOUR WEAPON!" Dale yelled.

Polk continued firing. Hagerty and his team reached Dale and Bowman.

"What in the blazin' hell is going on?" Hagerty asked.

"Very funny," Dale said.

Polk hit one of Hagerty's deputies in the leg by a bullet ricochet. Polk ran out of ammo. Dale and Bowman moved to the right side of the building. Hagerty moved to the left. Dale could faintly see Polk against the wall in the corner.

"Drop your gun!" Dale ordered.

Polk still had the gun in his hand. He knew he was through. Dale had his gun pointed at Polk. Hagerty had his revolver aimed at Polk from the left side. There was no way he could get out of that situation.

"FUCK YOU!" Polk yelled. He raised his gun at Dale.

Hagerty shot Polk in the chest. The shot threw Polk against the wall. Dale looked at Hagerty. He was in a state of shock. He had never shot anybody before. Dale walked over to him. He grabbed Hagerty's gun out of his hand.

"It's okay, Sheriff," Dale said to him.

Dale walked over to Polk. He checked for a pulse. He was dead. "Get the fire department in here," Dale said to Bowman.

Stephanie could smell the smoke coming from the factory. She ran to look out the window. She saw a fire truck pulling up. "HELP! UP HERE!" she screamed. They couldn't hear her.

Jensen busted the door open and walked over to Tyler. He took out a gun and pointed it at him. "LEAVE HIM ALONE!" she shouted.

"Get over here and sit down, or your new friend over there is going to have some company," Jensen said.

Stephanie walked over to the couch and sat next to Tyler. Jensen sat on the edge of the couch with his gun pointed at Tyler. Stephanie was shaking in fear. She knew this was it.

"Remember, this is all your fault. His blood his on your hands," Jensen said to her.

"And your blood is going to be on her hands, clothes, the walls, and the floor," Jack said as he walked into the office. "Drop it."

"Detective Prescott," Jensen said. He smiled at him. "He told us you would come eventually."

"Well, I'm glad I can live up to his standards. Drop the gun please," Jack said.

Jack aimed his gun at Jensen. Jensen wasn't moving. He still had his gun aimed at Tyler's head. Stephanie was paused. She didn't know what to do.

"I will decorate this room with this kid's fucking brains. Drop your gun," Jensen said.

They were at a standoff. Jack had a clear shot at Jensen. He didn't want to take the risk of him shooting Tyler. Jack slowly walked closer to toward the couch.

Stephanie took out the letter opener that she had in her sock. She was hiding it in her back pocket. She did it slowly to not attract attention from Jensen.

Jack saw what she was doing. He slowly lowered his gun down. "What do you want with them?" Jack asked.

"The big boss paid us. I don't ask questions. I just do what I'm paid to do," Jensen replied. "Just like you. You're paid to find the girl and kid."

"What did you do to the guy in the parking garage?"

"Oh, that's water under the bridge. There's more to this than you know, Detective."

"Well, why don't you tell me?" Jack asked.

"Oh, in time, in time."

Stephanie swung as hard as she could and stabbed Jensen in the leg with the letter opener. He screamed at the top of his lungs. He turned and hit Stephanie with his gun.

Jack ran over and attacked Jensen. They wrestled to the ground. Stephanie grabbed Tyler and went over by the door. She watched them struggle on the floor. Jack and Jensen got back up and wrestled up against a wall.

Jensen punched Jack in the face. He went to the floor. Jensen kicked him over and over again. He picked him and threw him over the desk. Jensen walked over and picked up his gun and walked over toward the desk.

Jack was on the floor behind desk. Jensen walked by the window and aimed his gun at Jack. "Goodbye, Detective Prescott," Jensen said.

Stephanie ran over to Jensen and pushed him out the window. She screamed at the top of her lungs as she lunged at him. He fell out the window screaming. She looked out the window and saw Jensen hit the ground.

Jack lied there on the floor in disbelief. She was at her breaking point. Everything that had happened to her in the last week, she just snapped. Jack got up and walked over to the window with Stephanie. She was breathing heavily as she stared down at Jensen's body.

"It's okay," Jack said to her. He put his hand on her back. She started crying. Jack embraced her. "C'mon," he said to her.

They walked over to the office door where Tyler was standing. They walked out of the building.

Protective Custody

Cappy and Sims raced to Bradley Community Hospital where they took Stephanie and Tyler. He was anxious to see how they were doing and wanted to make sure they were safe.

They pulled up to the entrance of the hospital and saw an FYNY news van parked in front. "How the hell did they get here before us?" Sims asked.

"Who cares?" Cappy replied.

They got out of the car and went inside. Cappy walked down the hallway and saw Andrea Bailey talking to Jack. Jack saw Cappy walk in. He didn't look too thrilled.

"I'll talk to you later," Jack said to her.

"I'm going live," she said as she walked out of the hospital.

Cappy walked over to Jack. "How are they doing?" he asked.

"Pretty shaken up. They went through a lot," Jack said.

"Any physical harm?"

"Mostly mental. They killed Jeremy Goldstein and tossed his body in the office where they were held. She saved my life. Pushed Jensen out the window. The local sheriff got Polk."

"So Polk and Jensen killed Jeremy?" Cappy asked.

"Nope, there's a fourth suspect. Possibly more."

"Jesus Christ! We need to put an end to this shit," Cappy said.

"We found them. That's all that matters."

"Marshal Davidson is on his way here now. They're going to move them to both to federal protective custody. You and Dale can follow up with trying to find who was behind this."

"Even if we did, not much evidence to go on. Whoever is behind this is good at covering his tracks."

"Nobody is perfect. They always leave something behind. That's where you come in," Cappy said sarcastically.

"I'm going to go check on them."

"I'm going to go talk to the press. Since she already got her exclusive," Cappy said

Jack couldn't pull one over Cappy's eyes. He may have been under a lot of stress, but he knew his children. At this point, he didn't care how Jack got his information. All he cared about was getting Stephanie and Tyler safe.

Jack walked into Stephanie's room. She was sitting on the edge of the bed with her head down. He walked over to her and sat next to her on her bed. He put his hand on her back.

"How are you holding up?" he asked.

"Have you ever felt that your life was nothing but an endless nightmare?" she asked.

"Lately, yes. But after finding you, it's not so bad."

She looked up at him and smiled. "Thank you, Detective. You saved my life."

"You saved mine," Jack replied with a smile.

"We're going to get you and Tyler checked out, then we're going to move you."

"Where?" she asked.

"I don't know. The US marshals are on their way and they'll explain it all to you."

"I want you to come with us," Stephanie said.

"I can't."

"I just feel so much safer with you around. I don't want to go through anything like that again."

"I understand. We still don't know who or why these guys were after you. I got to stay and find them. You'll be fine."

Jack got up and walked out of her room. He walked down the hallway and saw Dale sitting outside of Tyler's room. He sat down next to him. "How's he doing?" Jack asked.

"No physical injuries. But he's probably going to have some mental issues for a while."

"That kid saw man murdered in front of him then was chased by the same man, got kidnapped, and saw another dead body lying in front of him for God knows how long, not to mention the life he had before all this. But we did find them. That's the most important thing."

"What happens now?" Dale asked.

"Waiting for the marshals. They're going to move them to witness protection."

"What's our next move?" Dale asked.

"Well, first we're going to get something to eat, then have a drink. Or maybe twenty. Then get some sleep. Tomorrow we find the fucker in charge of this operation and maybe find the rat that helped them."

"You still think we have a rat in our department?"

"Pop is in denial about it. Too much points to there being a dirty cop."

Jack looked down the hallway and saw Marshal Davidson go into Stephanie's room. He felt relieved knowing she would finally be safe. But he still wasn't fully satisfied. He was determined to find the person behind their kidnappings.

Dale reached into his pocket and pulled out his pills. Jack looked over and watched him as he took one. He didn't fully trust Dale. He saw many people in pain and getting hooked on painkillers. He didn't want to see that happen to Dale.

"How's your side?" Jack asked.

"Not too bad. Don't worry, I only took one," Dale replied.

Davidson came out of Stephanie's room and walked down the hallway toward them. Jack was anxious to hear the good news that was to come.

"Good work, guys. I am impressed," Davidson said.

"What happens now?" Dale asked.

"We're going to move her and the kid into federal protective custody. There's a red-eye leaving for Miami tonight. We'll escort them there and relocate them."

"Well, that's good news," Jack said. "C'mon, partner, let's get out of here."

"Whoa! Where are you going?" Davidson said to Jack.

"Umm, I'm going to get a big-ass burger and some sleep."

"Unfortunately, the burger is going to have to wait. You can get some sleep on the plane though," Davidson said.

Jack was confused. "What the hell are you talking about?" Jack asked.

"The girl insisted that I bring you along with us to Miami. I agreed to it."

"Well, un-agree to it," Jack said aggressively.

Cappy came walking around the corner. "What's going on?" he asked.

"The feds want to kidnap me now."

"I would like for Detective Prescott to accompany me, the girl, and the kid to Miami. Ms. Lambert would feel much better if he came with us."

"I would like to, but I have a multiple homicide to investigate," Jack said.

"You could use the sleep. You better pack, Detective."

Jack wasn't thrilled at all. He didn't want to leave. "Pop, c'mon. You know how I feel about flying. Plus, we need to find the person who did all this."

"Dale and Sims will be fine for a day while you go. That's an order."

"Meet us at JFK at ten," Davidson said.

Red-Eye

Jack met with Davidson at JFK. It was after nine o'clock when he got there. There was a white Learjet parked outside the hangar. There were three black SUVs parked by the hangar.

Jack got out of the car and walked toward the vehicles. He saw Marshal Davidson get out of one of the SUVs. He walked over to Jack and extended his hand out. "Detective Prescott, welcome to JFK."

Jack was staring at the Learjet. He hated to fly. His stomach was in knots just looking at the plane. "So how fast does that thing go?" he asked.

"Oh, roughly around six hundred miles an hour," Davidson said.

Jack felt nauseous. He didn't want to go. "Let's get this shit over with," Jack said.

"Oh no. We're not going on this," Davidson said. "This is part of our routine with cases like these. We can't take a chance that somebody is watching us. One of the perks of being a part of witness protection, we blend in. It makes it harder to be found."

"So we're not flying to Miami?" Jack asked.

"Oh, we're still flying. And no, not to Miami. I only said that to throw people off. I don't trust anybody. That includes you."

Davidson walked over to one of the SUVs and opened the back door. Stephanie and Tyler both got out. She smiled at Jack. He returned one back at her.

"Shall we?" Davidson asked.

They all started walking toward the Atlantic Terminal. Stephanie walked beside Jack as she was holding Tyler's hand. "Thank you so much for coming."

"You're welcome," Jack replied.

Jack felt like he had been walking a marathon. They walked through the terminal to the security station. Davidson showed security his badge. They each went through the metal detector. Security was double since 9/11.

After being cleared, they all went to the waiting area. Jack walked over to the window and saw a jumbo jet. It was a 747. It was a dark gray jet with *Trans-Atlantic* along the side in blue lettering. "That's our ride," Davidson said. "I'm going to get our tickets."

Jack stood there staring out the window. He saw Tyler in the reflection of the window. He was staring outside beside him. "Have you ever been on a plane before?" Jack asked.

Tyler didn't say anything. Jack kneeled down next to him. "I've never been one on either," Jack said to Tyler.

"I'm scared," Tyler said.

Jack walked over to the chairs by the windows. Tyler walked over and sat beside him. "It's okay to be scared. I'm scared too."

"You're scared?" Tyler asked.

"Oh yeah. I was scared when the bad men took you and Stephanie. I was scared when I couldn't find you. But you know what? I just thought positive. Just keep thinking everything will be okay. Or think of something that makes you happy."

"What makes you happy?" Tyler asked.

"Why don't you go back and sit with Stephanie?" Jack said hesitantly.

He got up and went back over and sat with Stephanie. Davidson walked over to Jack. "How are you holding up?" he asked.

"Sore, tired, beat-up, tired of being blown up. The usual."

"Talked to the airline. They start boarding at midnight. They're letting us on an hour early."

"So where are we going?" Jack asked.

"Seattle. We'll relocate them there and give them new identities. We'll have a marshal assigned to them if anything were to happen. Any new leads on who did this?"

"He's smart. Every time we get one step behind this guy, he takes three steps forward."

"You think it's another dirty cop?" Davidson asked.

Jack looked surprised that Davidson knew what he was thinking. "I read about you and that Badger case. It's okay, I despise dirty cops too. That's why I didn't say anything in front of your captain."

"Cappy isn't dirty," Jack said.

"How can you be so sure?"

"He saved me and raised me since I was a teenager."

"So you mean he has never kept anything from you? Or you have never kept anything from him?"

Jack had nothing to say to that. He knew Davidson was right. He wished he weren't right. He still trusted him.

"Are you telling me not to trust him?" Jack asked.

"No. I'm telling you to be careful on who you trust. You trusted Lieutenant Tackler and look what happened. I've been doing this a long time, Jack. Just be careful is all."

Jack had a defeated look on his face. He knew deep down in his gut that somebody in his unit was behind this. He just couldn't face it.

"Don't worry. I'll take care of hiding our witnesses and you concentrate on finding the pricks who did it."

Davidson was supportive of Jack. Usually in these cases, the federal government shows no compassion with professional courtesy.

Jack just hoped that when he gets back, he can solve this case.

Takeoff

It was nearly eleven o'clock. Jack was getting anxious about getting on the plane. Tyler was sleeping on Stephanie's lap. Davidson was talking to the ticket agent by the ramp door. He walked over to Jack

"It's time," he said.

Jack got up and got his bag and waited for Stephanie and Tyler. They walked over to him. Stephanie was nervous. Tyler was tired and didn't know what was going on.

"Ready?" Davidson asked.

He walked down onto the entrance ramp to the plane. Stephanie and Tyler followed. Jack was hesitant to follow. "Fuck it," he said and walked through the ramp to the plane.

He walked onto the plane and was greeted by a young dark-haired flight attendant. He handed her his ticket. "You're in first-class, sir. It's up the stairs," she said.

Jack was surprised. He walked up the spiral staircase to the upper deck. He had never seen an airplane so spacious. The seats were as big as recliners. Dark gray seats with blue headrests and armrests.

"One good thing about being a fed, we always fly first-class," Davidson said to Jack with a smirk on his face.

Jack put his bag in the overhead storage compartment and sat down in his seat. Stephanie and Tyler sat to the right of Jack by the window. Davison sat on the left of Jack by the window.

Jack fastened his seat belt and grabbed his armrests. He was breathing heavy. Davidson looked over at him and smirked. Davidson flew all the time. It was a routine for him.

Tyler had the window seat. He was staring out the window as he was watching the planes take off and land as they waited their turn.

"How are you doing?" Stephanie asked.

Tyler looked over at her. "I don't want to be scared anymore," he said.

"Don't worry, sweetie. I'm not going to let anything happen to you."

"Will you be with me forever?" Tyler asked.

She didn't know what to say. She couldn't lie to him. "I can't promise you that. But I can promise that I'll make sure you're safe and happy."

"I found out the hard way to never make promises you can't keep," Jack said.

Stephanie looked over at him. "Me too. I promised myself I would be a better person after what I did."

"What did you do?" Jack asked.

"I made a lot of mistakes. I was a drug addict. I dated this drug dealer for like a month. He was warm to me, but cold to everybody else. He got me pregnant. I couldn't keep his baby. I gave it up for adoption the day he was born. I ran away and got myself clean. I got a job with DCFPS and have been doing that ever since."

"We won't let you down again," Jack said.

"I know. Maybe this is life's twisted way of my past coming back to haunt me. I see heartbreak and sadness on a daily basis. I took this job because I didn't want people feeling how I felt when I was with that drug dealer—empty, betrayed, sad, abused, the feeling of not being safe in your home."

"I see it every day too. How people are so cruel to one another. So much hatred in the world. Unfortunately, we get a ringside view of it. You can't change the world for the better. The only thing I hope for is that the world can change me for the better."

She smiled at him. It was rare that she does that. She never had the time to talk to somebody else about the hardships of their jobs or have somebody make her feel better.

Several minutes went by. Jack was getting more anxious. He was tapping his foot off the floor.

"Detective hotshot over there doesn't like to fly," Davidson said.

A flight attendant came upstairs to check on them. She was young and had her brunette hair in a ponytail. "Hello, I'm Amanda. I'll be your attendant for this evening. We will be getting ready to taxi in just a few minutes."

She walked to the back of the cabin. Davidson leaned over to Jack. "Don't worry, they have plenty of vomit bags."

"Go fuck yourself," Jack said back.

Amanda came back to the front of the cabin with a seat belt in her hand. "The head flight attendant will be on the intercom momentarily."

"Good evening, ladies and gentlemen. Welcome aboard to Trans-Atlantic flight 1586 nonstop from New York to Seattle. Please pay attention to the front of the cabin as your flight attendants demonstrate how to fasten your seat belts. Please use the card in the back of the seat in front of you to properly use your seat belt and to learn the safety features of our 747. If for any reason the plane should depressurize, an oxygen mask will automatically drop. The card also shows how to apply it should an emergency occur. Your seat cushion can also be used for a flotation device. We will be taxiing to the runway in just a few moments."

Jack could feel the plane backing up. He was breathing heavy. "Are you okay, sir?" Amanda asked.

"I'm just peachy, thanks," Jack replied.

Davidson was trying not to laugh. Tyler was looking out the window, watching as the plane was moving toward the runway. "You doing okay, sweetie?" Stephanie asked.

Tyler grabbed her hand.

"Do you want me to hold your hand too?" Stephanie asked Jack.

He looked over at her with a disgusted look on his face.

"Just kidding," she said.

The plane came to a stop.

"That wasn't so bad," Jack said.

"We didn't even take off yet, hotshot," Davidson said.

"OH FUCK!" he said out loud.

"Good evening, ladies and gentlemen. This is Captain Reynolds speaking. We're lined up for takeoff. We're just waiting on clearance from the tower. I'll be back to make an announcement once we're airborne."

Jack could hear the engines getting louder. The cabin started to vibrate. He looked over and saw the plane moving down the runway. Jack closed his eyes and was breathing heavier. His seat tilted back. He felt his stomach drop like he did riding a roller coaster.

He felt a rumble underneath him. He grabbed his armrests and held them tight.

"Relax, it's just the landing gear," Davidson said.

"You can open your eyes now," Stephanie said.

Jack slowly opened his eyes. "See, you're still here, hotshot," Davidson said.

"Yeah, I'd rather be on the ground, finding douchebags who made me come up here. Hopefully my partner is having better luck than me."

Loose Ends

Dale and Sims went back to the precinct with Cappy. They were hoping to get a jump-start on the investigation while Jack was in the air. Dale's side was hurting more than usual. He was trying to hide the pain from Cappy. At this point, he didn't think Cappy would even care about it.

"Bring the case files to my office. We're missing something," Cappy said aggressively.

Cappy stormed into his office. Sims and Dale looked at each other. "What's his issue?" Sims asked

"I think this case is getting to him. With Internal Affairs breathing down his neck and the stress of dead end after dead end, this was the wrong case to come back to. How's Kennedy?"

"Talked to him earlier. He's fine. Just pissed he's stuck in a hospital bed while we do all the work."

They grabbed their files and went into Cappy's office. He had his whiteboard up in the corner of his office. "Okay, let's start from scratch," Cappy said.

Sims and Dale both sat at the table in Cappy's office. They opened their files on the case.

"Stephanie Lambert, social worker for the Department of Children and Family Protective Services," Dale said.

"Claims that her date was murdered in front of her and then was being chased by the assailants," Sims added.

Cappy was writing details down on the board. "That would give them reason to want to kill her, not kidnap her. What about the kid?"

"We don't know. She tells us that she needs to see him at St. Catherine's. We get there, and the kid is being chased by a man dressed as a priest."

"We thinking it's the same killer?" Cappy asked.

"All signs pointed to it. They kidnapped both her and the kid," Sims added. "They didn't kill them. So whoever hired these guys wanted them for some reason."

"Yeah, that's what we have to find out," Cappy said. "Jesus Christ! I've been wearing this badge for nearly thirty years. I've dealt with my fair share of killers who think they're smarter than us. Let's assume this guy is not God and he's a human that makes mistakes. What are we missing?"

"We checked Keith Warrick's financials and phone logs. We know that Dulaney was being paid off. His payment was from the Cayman's. No way to trace it from the source," Dale said.

Cappy's phone was ringing. He walked over to his desk and answered it. "Homicide."

Sims and Dale were waiting anxiously to see who he was talking to. Cappy had a surprised look on his face. "We'll be right there," he said.

He hung up the phone. "Let's go," he said.

Sims and Dale looked at each other. "What's going on?" Sims asked.

Cappy didn't say anything and raced to the elevators. Dale and Sims followed.

Cappy drove to the morgue. "What's going on, Cappy?" Sims asked

"I think we're about to find out," he replied.

They got out of the car and walked into the morgue. It was after midnight. Dale and Sims followed Cappy down to the morgue. They were all physically spent. They walked in and saw Bones working on a body.

"Nice to see you again, Detective," 'Bones said to Dale.

"Always a pleasure, Bones," Dale said.

"What do you have for us?" Cappy asked.

"Captain Pinelli, it's been awhile. Glad to see you with your badge again. They found this man in the Hudson a few hours ago."

"What does this have to with us or our case?" Dale asked.

Bones walked over to the body. He uncovered it. Dale and Sims walked over to the table. Cappy walked over next to Bones. They all had a look at the body.

"Cause of death, a single stab wound to the left side of the chest. There was no water in his lungs, so he was dead before he was dumped."

"Sounds like our missing Derek Conway," Dale added.

"No actually," Bones said.

"What the hell do you mean no?" Cappy asked. "He resembles our sketch of what Stephanie described him as. She said she saw him get stabbed in the chest. What is the fuckin' problem?"

"His name, Captain."

Cappy looked dumbfounded. "You figured out his name? What's the big deal?"

"Lady and gentlemen, meet Mr. Ronald Logan."

Dale, Sims, and Cappy all looked at one another. They were all puzzled on what Bones just told them.

"How can that be?" Sims asked. "They found his blood at the crime scene. He ran and got his file."

"The blood was only run through the state archives. Everybody I examine, I run their prints through the local, state, federal, and Interpol databanks. Then talked to the people over at technical assistance. They told me your Ronald Logan was a fake. Somebody put a fake file in the computer to throw you offtrack would be my guess."

"So who is the real Ronald Logan?" Cappy asked.

Bones walked over to his desk and came back with his file. "I didn't have a chance to go through it yet."

Cappy took the file and was looking through it. "He was an FBI informant," Cappy said.

He handed the file to Dale. "Look who his contact agent was," Cappy said to Dale.

"Fuck. Agent Mike Temple."

"Yes, Agent Temple," Bones added. "I just happened to have his file as well."

"How the hell you get an agents personnel file?" Cappy asked.

"It's weird dealing with the dead all the time and have time to get scoop on somebody living. I have people in high places. A colleague of mine is a medical examiner in Washington."

He handed the file to Cappy. He took it and looked through it. "Agent Mike Temple. Did a tour in Desert Storm. Honorable discharge. Demolition expert."

"So it had to have been Temple who put the fake file in the computer," Sims said.

"I bet he was the one following us all over the city too. And the one who put the bomb in the microwave. I bet he's our big boss," Dale added.

"What's the plan, Cappy?" Dale asked.

"I think it's time we go pay Agent Temple a visit," Cappy said. "Here's his address. Good seeing you again, Doc."

"Always a pleasure," Bones said.

Cappy raced back up to the car. Dale and Sims followed. "Looks like the trail got warm again," Dale said.

"It's time to end this fucking thing," Cappy said.

Partners in Crime

Cappy, Dale, and Sims got to Temple's apartment after 1:00 AM. "I know that car," Dale said. There was a black Chevy Caprice parked outside of Temple's apartment building.

"What car?" Sims asked.

"That car was following me and Jack all over the city, looking for these guys. Was even there when we raided that halfway house before it blew up."

"What's the plan, Cappy?" Sims asked.

Cappy looked at Temple's car and then back up at his apartment building. "Fuck it!" Cappy got out of the car and walked into the building. Dale and Sims followed.

"I don't think he's in the right state of mind," Sims said.

"Me either, but what other choice do we have?" Dale asked.

Cappy walked up to the second floor to Temple's apartment. He drew his gun out. Dale and Sims got up to the second floor and saw Cappy halfway down the hallway, standing outside of Temple's apartment. They walked down to him and drew their guns as well.

Cappy knocked on the door. There was no answer. Cappy knocked again. "Agent Temple? It's Captain Pinelli. We need to talk."

There was still no answer. Cappy looked down the hallway. He kicked open the door. Dale and Sims didn't know what to think. They didn't have a warrant.

"Cappy! What the hell are you doing?" Dale asked.

Cappy was searching Temple's apartment. Dale and Sims just stood there, watching. He was like a man possessed. Cappy reminded

Dale of Jack. He just let Cappy do his thing. He walked into the bedroom.

"You guys better get back here," Cappy yelled.

Dale and Sims looked at each other and walked back to the bedroom. They walked in and saw Cappy standing over the body of Agent Temple. He had been shot in the head.

"Point-blank between the eyes," Cappy said as he stared over Temple's body. "Apparently he knew too much."

"I'm getting really fucking tired of this dead-body crap," Dale said. "Every time we get close, it ends up a dead end."

"Look around. See if Agent Temple left us anything useful," Cappy demanded.

Dale and Sims went out and searched Temple's apartment. Dale was hoping they'd find something that would help them. He was now feeling what Jack felt on a daily basis. No clues and nothing but dead bodies.

Cappy came out from the bedroom with a photo album. He sat down on the couch and started to look through it.

"You really think you're going to find something in there?" Sims asked.

"You never know anymore," Cappy said as he scrolled through the album. He stopped on and studied a picture. "You know this guy?" he asked Dale.

Dale walked over to the couch and sat next to Cappy. Cappy took out the picture and handed it to Dale.

"SON OF A BITCH!" Dale said.

"I take it you know him?" Cappy asked.

"Yeah, I do."

Sims walked over to the couch. "Well, who the hell is he?" she asked.

"It's Agent Temple standing next to Todd Markus. He's Stephanie's boss at DCFPS."

"That's no coincidence," Cappy said.

"Let's go have a chat with Mr. Boss Man," Cappy said.

They left Temple's apartment and walked down the hallway. A man walked up to them. "I'm the manager. Can I help you?"

"NYPD," Cappy said to him. "Call the police and tell them to go to Agent Temple's place. He's been killed."

"Oh shit," the manager said. "I should go and let Mr. Markus know."

Cappy grabbed the manager's arm as he was walking away. "Whoa! Mr. Markus?" Cappy asked. "As in Todd Markus?"

"Yes, Todd Markus. He lives one floor up."

"How do you know that Agent Temple and Markus are acquainted?" Dale asked.

"Markus is Agent Temple's ex-brother-in-law."

"What room is Markus in?" Cappy asked.

"He's in room 308," the manager said.

They rushed up to Markus's room. They had their guns out. Dale kicked down the door.

"NYPD!" Cappy yelled.

There was no sign of Markus. "Well, no dead body. That's a plus," Sims said.

"We had the motherfucker. He was under our noses the entire time," Dale said.

"Look around. Has to be something here." Cappy was getting agitated. He felt he didn't have the edge anymore. He needed this case to come to its conclusion.

"Hey, I found something," Sims said. She came out into the living room with a piece of paper. They all looked at it. *Fifteen eighty-six* was written on the paper.

"Jesus fuckin' Christ! He's on the plane!" Cappy said.

Turbulence

Nearly an hour into the flight, Jack was still clinched to his seat. The plane was experiencing turbulence. "This shit needs to stop!"

"Oh hush, puppy. It's just a little turbulence," Davidson said.

Amanda walked by. "Would anybody like anything to drink?" she asked.

"Yeah, some Pepto-Bismol." Jack was getting pale as the plane was rocking through the rough air.

"Are you okay, sir?" she asked.

"Just not a fan of flying. How much longer is the flight?"

"About four more hours."

Jack rolled his eyes. He was hoping that she was going to say another five minutes. The plane was rocking back and forth.

"Is this normal?" Jack asked.

"We're heading into a storm. Don't worry. I've flown through dozens of storms. There's nothing to worry about."

Amanda's reassurance was helping Jack calm down. He wasn't breathing as hard. Davidson looked over at him and shook his head in disbelief. "You going to make it?" he asked.

"I'll be fine once this thing is on the ground."

"You'll be okay then. About four hours from now," Davidson said.

Jack leaned his head back against the headrest. Stephanie looked over at him. "It'll be okay, Detective."

"Yeah, it'll be okay," Tyler said.

Jack looked over to make sure he heard correctly. Tyler spoke to him. He smiled at him. That made him feel even more better. "Yeah, it will be," he said back to Tyler.

"Detective Prescott?" Amanda asked.

"Now what?" he replied.

"We have a call patched through the cockpit for you."

Jack looked over at Davidson. "Who the hell is calling me at thirty-five thousand feet?"

Jack unsnapped his seat belt and walked with Amanda to the cockpit. "What's going on?" Jack asked.

The captain handed Jack the headset. "We have him patched in from JFK."

"Who?" Jack asked.

"He didn't say except it was urgent."

The plane was being rocked by the storm. Jack could hear the thunder outside of the plane. The flashes of lightning were making him more nervous.

"This is Prescott."

"It's Cappy. We have a big problem."

"What now?" he asked.

"We found out who is after Stephanie and Tyler?"

"Who?"

"Her boss. Todd Markus."

"You got to be shitting me," Jack said.

"He's Agent Temple's ex-brother-in-law. They were in it together. They set the whole thing up. Markus and Temple hired Warrick and the others. We found a body in the Hudson. It was Robert Logan. Temple put a fake file in the computer to throw us offtrack. Temple is also an expert in explosives."

"Did you find them?"

"Markus killed Temple. He's on the plane with you."

Jack took off the headset. "How soon can you land this thing?"

"You have a legitimate reason for wanting to land?" Captain Reynolds asked.

"How about a kidnapper and killer on board?"

Reynolds looked over at his copilot. The plane was bouncing through the storm.

"This storm is an issue."

"How long?" Jack asked.

"It's hard to say," Reynolds said.

"How long?"

"Chicago is our best bet. We're about forty minutes south of O'Hare."

"Get it on the ground."

Jack walked out of the cockpit. He walked over to talk to Davidson. He was sleeping in his seat. "How the fuck can he be sleeping through this shit?"

He shook him. "I need to talk to you," Jack said.

Davidson didn't wake up. Jack shook him harder. He looked behind him to see if Stephanie was watching him. She was looking out the window while Tyler slept. Jack checked his pulse. He was still alive.

"You were drugged," Jack said to Davidson.

He walked over to Stephanie and Tyler. "Wake him up," Jack demanded.

"Why? He finally went to sleep, surprisingly with all these bumps from the storm."

Jack reached across her and shook Tyler. "Hey, buddy, wake up," Jack said.

Tyler didn't move. Stephanie reached across and tapped him on the leg. "Wake up, sweetie," she said.

"Tyler! What happened to him?" she frantically asked.

Jack picked up Stephanie's glass and looked at it. He squinted his eyes. He held the glass up to the light. There was a powered substance floating at the bottom of her drink.

"They were drugged."

"They?" Stephanie asked.

"Davidson is out too," Jack said as he looked over at him. The storm was making Jack a wreck. The lights on the plane were flickering.

"How were they drugged?" Stephanie asked.

Jack stood back up. He looked around. Looked at Davidson and then back over at Tyler. "Amanda!"

He walked to the back of the first-class cabin to talk to Amanda. He pulled open the curtain. She wasn't there. He knocked on the lavatory door. "Amanda? You in there?" He opened the door. It was empty.

Jack could feel the plane turning. He had to find Markus before he realizes Jack was on to him. He went down the stairs to the main cabins. The plane felt like a bumpy roller-coaster ride. Jack had to hold on tight to the railing.

He was trying to be discreet. Amanda was nowhere to be found. He walked to the main galley and saw a male flight attendant "Excuse me? Have you seen Amanda?" he asked.

"Yes, sir. She went down below deck to help prep the meals. Is there something I can help you with?" the flight attendant asked.

"No, thanks."

He peeked his head behind the curtain to have a full view of the main cabin. He was trying to look for Markus. Most of the passengers in the cabin were sleeping. He walked slowly back into the cabin. He looked at each passenger as he walked by. Markus wasn't there.

Jack held on to each seat as the turbulence rocked the plane. The lightning outside the windows lit up the inside of the plane. He made his way back to the coach cabin. Markus was not anywhere to be found.

He walked back up to the front of the plane. "Oh, sir, Amanda just went back upstairs with a gentleman," the male flight attendant said.

"Gentleman?" Jack asked.

"Yes. Some guy wanted to use the lavatory upstairs. It's not unusual for a passenger to want to go upstairs on our 747s, especially the ones with bars."

Jack slowly walked up the stairs to the first-class cabin. When we got to the top of the steps, he saw Markus. He was pointing a gun at Stephanie and Tyler. "Give your gun to her, or I kill her right here right now," Markus said.

Amanda was standing next to Jack with her hand out. She was in on it with him. Jack slowly reached under his shirt and pulled out his Glock. Amanda took it out of his hands and pointed it at him.

"It was you the whole time, huh?" Jack asked.

"Ha ha, he said you were good," Markus said.

The storm was getting worse. The plane was rocking more. The seat belt sign came on. Jack was holding on to the rail from the steps. He was getting nauseous.

"Oh, Mr. Almighty NYPD Tough Guy is afraid of flying, huh?"

"He's been crying like a baby since takeoff," Amanda said.

"Nah, it's that horrible smell," Jack said. He started sniffing around. "Oh, it's you," he said to Amanda with a smirk on his face.

She smacked him in the head with his own gun. Markus smiled as Jack went to the floor. Stephanie was in tears. Tyler and Davidson were still unconscious.

"You know, I'm really getting sick and fuckin' tired of getting my ass kicked and blown up. So before the streak continues, tell me why."

"I can't go into the details, but our little social worker here has quite the past. Unfortunately, her crimes are punishable by death. Me, along with my ex-wife, Amanda, over there, and others, tried to collect her and the boy."

"What has the kid done?" Jack asked.

"I asked my boss the same question. I'll tell you the same thing he told me: it's personal."

"Well, now that you have us all here, thirty thousand feet above solid ground, why don't you tell me who your boss is?"

"The money he paid me, I'm not at liberty to say. But you will find out soon enough," Markus said.

"So what happens now?" Jack asked.

"You and Amanda are going to go into the cockpit and tell the captain to change course back to New York. By then, the drugs will wear off. Me, Stephanie, and the kid are going to get off and disappear into the crowd."

The plane jerked. Jack threw up on the floor. Amanda stepped away from him. She kept his gun on him. "I'm tired of this turbulence," Jack said.

"That was the landing gear," Amanda said.

"Go tell them to get us back in the air," Markus ordered.

Amanda went to the cockpit. He banged on the door. "GET US BACK IN THE AIR!" she screamed. Jack slowly reached down to get his revolver from his ankle holster. The pilots didn't answer.

Markus was watching Amanda at the cockpit door. Stephanie looked back at Jack and saw him reaching for his revolver. She nodded her head at him. Jack slowly drew his gun. Stephanie quickly looked out the window and saw the lights of Chicago getting bigger.

Jack could feel the plane slowing down as they were landing. Amanda was banging on the door. The pilots didn't answer. "TAKE US BACK UP!" Markus shouted.

Stephanie took a couple of deep breaths. Jack slowly got back up to his feet. Stephanie screamed and pushed Markus's arm away and his gun fired. He shot a window. The pressurization of the plane made the hole bigger.

The force of the wind from the storm and the plane was so fierce. The oxygen masks were deployed from the overhead.

"KEEP AHOLD OF TYLER!" Jack yelled at Stephanie. The wind was so loud that she couldn't hear him.

Markus was trying to balance himself. The plane was rocking back and forth, and he was fighting against the wind. Amanda was holding on to the cockpit door handle. Jack fought his way toward Stephanie's seat.

Markus turned and pointed his gun at Jack. "YOUR BLOOD IS ON HER HANDS!" he screamed at Jack.

Stephanie closed her eyes and embraced Tyler. She heard a gunshot. She opened her eyes and saw Markus standing by her with blood coming from his chest.

Amanda shot him. Jack had his gun on Markus. He went to the floor. Amanda still had Jack's Glock pointed at Markus. The plane hit the runway. The force of the plane landing knocked Amanda and Jack off their feet again.

Jack dropped his revolver as they hit the floor. Amanda got back up and pointed her gun at Stephanie. "THIS IS ALL YOUR FAULT!" she screamed at her. She aimed the gun at her. Stephanie closed her eyes and heard another gunshot.

She opened her eyes. Amanda hit the floor. She looked over at Jack. He didn't have his gun. Jack looked over and saw Davidson pointing his gun at her. Jack put his head down and sighed in relief.

Stephanie started crying again. Jack grabbed his revolver and stood up. He walked over to Stephanie. "Are you all right?" he asked.

She nodded her head yes as she wiped the tears off her cheek. "It's never going to end, is it?" she asked.

"It never does end," Jack bluntly said.

Jack could feel the plane slowing down. He walked over to Davidson. "You okay?" he asked.

"Have a massive headache," he said as he held his head.

"Welcome to my world," Jack replied.

Game Over

It was hours after the plane had landed at O'Hare. The sun was coming up. Stephanie was waiting for Tyler to wake up at the airport infirmary. She was sitting outside the office. She was at her wit's end. The last week felt like a lifetime of nonstop nightmares for her.

Jack came over and sat next to her. He was beat-up, tired, and everything in between. "Once the kid is cleared, the marshals are moving you," Jack told her.

"Same place?" she asked.

"No, Davidson has been on the phone for an hour. I won't even know your new location. You and Tyler will be safe."

"Safe? Ha ha! That's a good one. We will never be safe. The sad part is, I don't even know who is doing this."

Jack knew she was lying. Nobody goes through this much trouble over a social worker. It had to be connected to her past. They went through all her cases. Nothing came up.

"Their blood is on your hands?" Jack asked.

"What?"

"That's what Markus and Amanda said to you. Their blood is on your hands. The way that sounded is that they're blaming you for all these deaths. Why do you suppose that is?"

"I don't know what they meant. I've had a troubled past. I put that behind me and moved on to a better life."

"Yeah, well, apparently, your past came back with a vengeance."

Davidson came out of the infirmary. Stephanie got up and walked to him. "Is Tyler all right?" she asked.

"He's fine. A little weak and tired from the drugs, we got on the plane. We're going to be moving out in a few minutes."

Jack got up and walked to Davidson and Stephanie. "Well, Detective, what can I say?"

"How about sorry for making you get on a plane with a murderer? Maybe a thank-you for helping you feds out. Thank you for saving your ass?"

"How about kiss my ass?" Davidson asked.

Jack smirked. Davidson extended his hand out. Jack shook it.

"Thank you for everything, Detective," Davidson said.

"It was a fun game" Jack replied.

Davidson was puzzled. "Game?"

"Yeah, I've always considered my job a game. Good guys versus bad guys. Every case is a new game. The victims are safe and being put into protective custody. We're still sucking air. We won. They lost."

"That's a unique perspective, Prescott. But I will say this. You do play the game well."

"Well, it's like Motorhead says: it's all about the game and how you play it," Jack said.

"Isn't that Triple H's theme song?" Davidson asked.

"You watch pro wrestling too?"

"We'll save that for another time. We better get going," Davidson said to Stephanie.

"You take care of yourself," Jack said to her.

"Please find out who did this," she said to Jack.

"Don't worry, one way or another, we will find the man behind this."

Davidson and Stephanie walked down the hall. Tyler was waiting outside the infirmary with three other US marshals. Jack stood there and watched as they walked away. She grabbed Tyler's hand and looked back at Jack. She smiled at him.

He smiled back and waved at them. He watched them walk away and uttered, "Game over."

Plan B

Bo Murdock was an elite attorney. He was the best of the best when it came to high-profile trials. He was well-connected. He had the money and the resources to win in the courtroom.

He went to Riker's Island for a meeting with his client. He went in through the checkpoints with his leather briefcase and five-thousand-dollar suit with a cocky smile on his face.

He walked into the holding cell area. "My client is expecting me," he said to the guard.

He gave Murdock a visitor's pass and escorted him to a holding cell. He walked in and had a seat. His client was there waiting for him. He sat down and put his briefcase on the floor next to him.

"The plane landed in Chicago. Markus was killed," he said to his client.

"What about the girl and kid?" his client asked.

"They're now in witness protection. You were right about Prescott. He is good. What do we do now?" he asked.

He leaned in and whispered, "Plan B."

*****

It was two days later. Jack got back to the precinct. He was exhausted. His work wasn't done yet. He has not only a ton of paperwork to do but also a challenge to find out who was behind these murders.

He got off the elevator and walked into the squad room. Kennedy and Sims were sitting at their desks. "Look who's back," Jack said to Kennedy.

"It sucks to be back. Heard you had a little plane trouble."

"Go fuck yourself!"

"Boys, play nice now," Sims said. "How's the girl and kid?"

"Safe," Jack replied.

Dale was in Cappy's office. Jack didn't feel like waiting for him to be done. He walked in. Dale was sitting in front of Cappy's desk. Lieutenant Graham was sitting at the table.

"Oh, Detective Prescott. I'm glad to see you still in one piece. How was your flight?" he sarcastically asked.

"What the hell do you want?" Jack asked.

"Oh, I was just leaving actually. But I will say this, I really hope all your paperwork and accounts for what happened this past week are facts. I will be conducting a full investigation into this unit starting Monday. Good day, gentlemen."

Jack stared a hole right through Graham as he walked out of Cappy's office. Cappy knew Graham meant every word he said. "I need to talk to you—alone," Jack said.

Dale slowly got up and walked out to his desk. Jack closed the door behind Dale. He sat in the chair in front of Cappy's desk where Dale was sitting.

"How's the girl and kid?" Cappy asked.

"They're fine," he replied.

"How are you feeling?"

"Like shit. I'm exhausted, sore, tired of being shot at, and blown up. I should've been an action movie star. We have a problem."

"Just one, huh?" Cappy asked.

"Seriously, Pop, we have a rat."

Cappy made a fist and slammed it on his desk. "Quit saying that," he demanded.

"Why? You know it's true. Somebody has been helping whoever is behind all this shit the entire time. There's no way that there isn't a rat."

"You have any evidence?" Cappy asked.

"I have a hunch," Jack replied.

"Yeah, well, a hunch is just indigestion if you don't have any solid evidence."

"Well, hopefully Graham can find them in his little investigation."

"Who do you think it is?" Cappy asked.

Jack sighed heavily. He stood up in front of Cappy and looked out his office door window. He saw Dale, Sims, and Kennedy talking to one another. He turned and looked back at Cappy. "It's one of us."

Cappy put his head down. "Sweet fuckin' Jesus. Why is it I knew you were going to say that?"

"Because it's true," Jack said.

"This conversation doesn't leave this room. Understand?" Cappy asked.

"I got it. Going to go do paperwork until the end of the year."

Jack walked back out of the office and went to sit at his desk. He got out some forms to fill out. "You need anything?" Dale asked.

"Just to get this shit over with," Jack replied. "Oh well, it can't get any worse, right?"

"Detective Prescott?" asked a young woman walking into the squad room. Dale pointed at him from his desk.

"Over here," Jack said. "What did I do now?" he asked.

The lady gave him an envelope and walked away. They all watched her leave. "Who the hell was that?" Sims asked.

"An old flame suing you for alimony?" Kennedy asked.

Jack opened the envelope. He unfolded the document and looked at it. Jack had a shocked look on his face.

"Well?" Dale asked.

Jack didn't say anything. He just sat there at his desk, staring at the document.

Cappy came out of his office. "How's everybody doing?"

Everybody was looking over at Jack at his desk. Nothing was said. He was still staring at the document that was handed to him.

"What's going on?" Cappy asked.

"I've been summoned," Jack said.

"For what?" Dale asked.

"I've been summoned by Trent Kane to be a defense witness to his trial."

About the Author

Zach Peckens is a radiologic technologist at a local hospital. *Protective Custody* is the second crime novel he has written. James Patterson and Stephen King were Zach's inspiration to write books. He hopes to one day have one of his books on the *New York Times* best seller list.

CPSIA information can be obtained
at www.ICGtesting.com
Printed in the USA
LVHW030105090821
694770LV00004B/507